Washington Irving

The Legends of Sleepy Hollow

Paul Carro

Illustrations by Ananyo C

CONTENTS

INTRODUCTION

Washington Irving's *The Legend of sleepy Hollow* is an iconic horror tale. Many readers name the story as their gateway to horror books. I remember thinking as a kid, "Teacher's let us read this stuff?" Though my parents gave me a set bedtime every night, I did the flashlight under-the-covers thing to stay up late reading. It was under the covers of night and blanket that I first read about the terrifying headless horseman.

I assume most of you have already read the story and enjoy revisiting it. In the off chance *The Legend of Sleepy Hollow* is new to you, strap yourself in. The original story is reprinted here. But the book has been printed many times over. What makes this volume different? Well, Irving left some legends untold. Within the pages of his original story, Irving wrote about the Woman in White and a ghostly funeral train.

As a kid, I assumed he would tell those tales as well, so I searched for them but never found them anywhere. Now, as an adult, a fan, and a horror author, I thought it time to tell those untold stories. While writing them I tried to imagine how Irving might have told the tales.

Though those other legends percolated in my brain since childhood, I never considered putting pen to paper (or fingers to keyboard) until a recent series of fortunate events. (Hat tip to Lemony Snicket.) This book was born not only from my love of the source material, but because the Horror Writer's Association rejected me.

Allow me to explain.

Every year the Horror Writer's Association (of which I am a proud active member) produces an anthology tie-in with the Stoker awards. This was my first eligible year to submit, and the HWA picked a dinger of a theme: *Scaring and Daring Adventures.*

The parameters for submitting were to work with characters from a public domain work and approach it like the adventure books from years ago. This was perfect for me. Ichabod Crane immediately came to mind.

Even though I long wondered about The Woman in White and the Funeral Train, the direction I thought those stories might go differed from the HWA homework assignment. Rather than try to Frankenstein Monster those stories into an adventure tale, I came up with something totally new that still tied into the mythos.

What happened immediately after the original story? (Trying to avoid a hundred-year-old spoiler here.) That was the idea that became *The Many Legends of Sleepy Hollow.* I authored the submission story with great care and tried to remain true to the flavor and time-period of the original work.

In the end, I did not make the cut. Though HWA was very kind (I call it classy) in their rejection letter. I could never complain about the rejection because it is part of publishing, and I was competing against some of the best authors in the business. I was happy just to be shortlisted and intend to read that anthology when it comes out.

So how did this book you are holding come about from that rejection? Well, I put so much care into the submitted story that I hated to simply file it away never to be seen. With many stories, authors resubmit until it is published somewhere. Except this story was so niche it had no other natural home. Not exactly a perfect fit for more modern horror magazines and anthologies.

While considering my options, I revisited my ideas on the untold legends of the Hollow that I had long daydreamed about. With the love and appreciation that I held for Irving's work, I decided to write those untold stories. In doing so, I tried my best to lean into both Irving's style, and the intended reader's age. (So yes, kids of a certain age as well as adults can enjoy these new stories.)

As proof of my love for the source material, I previously published a story as an homage to *The Legend of Sleepy Hollow*. In that story, *The Candy House,* a teen riding a bike gets chased by something eager to behead him. I won't spoil it here. But it ties into Ichabod Crane's fascination with witchcraft. I felt the previously published story fit well with this book. While that one story is a modern take, the rest of the stories take place around the time of the original story and are set within the Hollow.

The last thing was to commission artwork reminiscent of the time. I am excited to have this out in the world and to see my name alongside this author from my childhood. I am equally excited to think someone might discover this classic tale for the first time, and hopefully enjoy my contributions to the Sleepy Hollow universe.

Welcome to *The Legend(s) of Sleepy Hollow*. Enjoy the book at your leisure, but I recommend reading it under the covers with a flashlight.

—Paul Carro

THE LEGEND OF SLEEPY HOLLOW

FOUND AMONG THE PAPERS OF THE LATE DIEDRICH KNICKERBOCKER.

A pleasing land of drowsy head it was,
Of dreams that wave before the half-shut eye;
And of gay castles in the clouds that pass,
Forever flushing round a summer sky.
CASTLE OF INDOLENCE.

In the bosom of one of those spacious coves which indent the eastern shore of the Hudson, at that broad expansion of the river denominated by the ancient Dutch navigators the Tappan Zee, and where they always prudently shortened sail and implored the protection of St. Nicholas when they crossed, there lies a small market town or rural port, which by some is called Greensburgh, but which is more generally and properly known by the name of Tarry Town. This name was given, we are told, in former days, by the good housewives of the adjacent country, from the inveterate propensity of their husbands to linger about the village tavern on market days. Be that as it may, I do not vouch for the fact, but merely advert to it, for the sake of being precise and authentic. Not far from this village, perhaps about two miles, there is a little valley or rather lap of land among high hills, which is one of the quietest places in the whole world. A small brook glides through it, with just murmur enough to lull one to repose; and the occasional whistle of a quail or tapping of a woodpecker is almost the only sound that ever breaks in upon the uniform tranquility.

I recollect that, when a stripling, my first exploit in squirrel-shooting was in a grove of tall walnut-trees that shades one side of the valley. I had wandered into it at noontime, when all nature is peculiarly quiet, and was startled by the roar of my own gun, as it broke the Sabbath stillness around and was prolonged and reverberated by the angry echoes. If ever I should wish for a retreat whither I might steal from the world and its distractions, and dream quietly away the remnant of a troubled life, I know of none more promising than this little valley.

From the listless repose of the place, and the peculiar character of its inhabitants, who are descendants from the original Dutch settlers, this sequestered glen has long been known by the name of SLEEPY HOLLOW, and its rustic lads are called the Sleepy Hollow Boys throughout all the neighboring country. A drowsy, dreamy influence seems to hang over the land, and to pervade the very atmosphere. Some say that the place was bewitched by a High German doctor, during the early days of the settlement; others, that an old Indian chief, the prophet or wizard of his tribe, held his powwows there before the country was discovered by Master Hendrick Hudson. Certain it is, the place still continues under the sway of some witching power, that holds a spell over the minds of the good people, causing them to walk in a continual reverie. They are given to all kinds of marvelous beliefs, are subject to trances and visions, and frequently see strange sights, and hear music and voices in the air. The whole neighborhood abounds with local tales, haunted spots, and twilight superstitions; stars shoot and meteors glare oftener across the valley than in any other part of the country, and the nightmare, with her whole ninefold, seems to make it the favorite scene of her gambols.

The dominant spirit, however, that haunts this enchanted region, and seems to be commander-in-chief of all the powers of the air, is the apparition of a figure on horseback, without a head. It is said by some to be the ghost of a Hessian trooper, whose head had been carried away by a cannon-ball, in some nameless battle during the Revolutionary War, and who is ever and anon seen by the country folk hurrying along in the gloom of night, as if on the wings of the wind. His haunts are not confined to the valley, but extend at times to the adjacent roads, and especially to the vicinity of a church at no great distance. Indeed, certain of the most authentic historians of those parts, who have been careful in collecting and collating the floating facts concerning this spectre, allege that the body of the trooper having been buried in the churchyard, the ghost rides forth to the scene of battle in nightly quest of his head, and that the rushing speed with which he sometimes passes along the Hollow, like a midnight blast, is owing to his being belated, and in a hurry to get back to the churchyard before daybreak.

Such is the general purport of this legendary superstition, which has furnished materials for many a wild story in that region of shadows; and the spectre is known at all the country firesides, by the name of the Headless Horseman of Sleepy Hollow.

It is remarkable that the visionary propensity I have mentioned is not confined to the native inhabitants of the valley, but is unconsciously imbibed by every one who resides there for a time. However wide awake they may have been before they entered that sleepy region, they are sure, in a little time, to inhale the witching influence of the air, and begin to grow imaginative, to dream dreams, and see apparitions.

I mention this peaceful spot with all possible laud, for it is in such little retired Dutch valleys, found here and there embosomed in the great State of New York, that population, manners, and customs remain fixed, while the great torrent of migration and improvement, which is making such incessant changes in other parts of this restless country, sweeps by them unobserved. They are like those little nooks of still water, which border a rapid stream, where we may see the straw and bubble riding quietly at anchor, or slowly revolving in their mimic harbor, undisturbed by the rush of the passing current. Though many years have elapsed since I trod the drowsy shades of Sleepy Hollow, yet I question whether I should not still find the same trees and the same families vegetating in its sheltered bosom.

In this by-place of nature there abode, in a remote period of American history, that is to say, some thirty years since, a worthy wight of the name of Ichabod Crane, who sojourned, or, as he expressed it, "tarried," in Sleepy Hollow, for the purpose of instructing the children of the vicinity. He was a native of Connecticut, a State which supplies the Union with pioneers for the mind as well as for the forest, and sends forth yearly its legions of frontier woodmen and country schoolmasters. The cognomen of Crane was not inapplicable to his person. He was tall, but exceedingly lank, with narrow shoulders, long arms and legs, hands that dangled a mile out of his sleeves, feet that might have served for shovels, and his whole frame most loosely hung together. His head was small, and flat at top, with huge ears, large green glassy eyes, and a long snipe nose, so that it looked like a weather-cock perched upon his spindle neck to tell which way the wind blew. To see him striding along the profile of a hill on a windy day, with his clothes bagging and fluttering about him, one might have mistaken him for the genius of famine descending upon the earth, or some scarecrow eloped from a cornfield.

His schoolhouse was a low building of one large room, rudely constructed of logs; the windows partly glazed, and partly patched with leaves of old copybooks. It was most ingeniously secured at vacant hours, by a tithe twisted in the handle of the door, and stakes set against the window shutters; so that though a thief might get in with perfect ease, he would find some embarrassment in getting out,--an idea most probably borrowed by the architect, Yost Van Houten, from the mystery of an eelpot. The schoolhouse stood in a rather lonely but pleasant situation, just at the foot of a woody hill, with a brook running close by, and a formidable birch-tree growing at one end of it. From hence the low murmur of his pupils' voices, conning over their lessons, might be heard in a drowsy summer's day, like the hum of a beehive; interrupted now and then by the authoritative voice of the master, in the tone of menace or command, or, peradventure, by the appalling sound of the birch, as he urged some tardy loiterer along the flowery path of knowledge. Truth to say, he was a conscientious man, and ever bore in mind the golden maxim, "Spare the rod and spoil the child." Ichabod Crane's scholars certainly were not spoiled.

I would not have it imagined, however, that he was one of those cruel potentates of the school who joy in the smart of their subjects; on the contrary, he administered justice with discrimination rather than severity; taking the burden off the backs of the weak, and laying it on those of the strong. Your mere puny stripling, that winced at the least flourish of the rod, was passed by with indulgence; but the claims of justice were satisfied by inflicting a double portion on some little tough wrong-headed, broad-skirted Dutch urchin, who sulked and swelled and grew dogged and sullen beneath the birch. All this he called "doing his duty by their parents;" and he never inflicted a chastisement without following it by the assurance, so consolatory to the smarting urchin, that "he would remember it and thank him for it the longest day he had to live."

When school hours were over, he was even the companion and playmate of the larger boys; and on holiday afternoons would convoy some of the smaller ones home, who happened to have pretty sisters, or good housewives for mothers, noted for the comforts of the cupboard. Indeed, it behooved him to keep on good terms with his pupils. The revenue arising from his school was small, and would have been scarcely sufficient to furnish him with daily bread, for he was a huge feeder, and, though lank, had the dilating powers of an anaconda; but to help out his maintenance, he was, according to country custom in those parts, boarded and lodged at the houses of the farmers whose children he instructed. With these he lived successively a week at a time, thus going the rounds of the neighborhood, with all his worldly effects tied up in a cotton handkerchief.

That all this might not be too onerous on the purses of his rustic patrons, who are apt to consider the costs of schooling a grievous burden, and schoolmasters as mere drones, he had various ways of rendering himself both useful and agreeable. He assisted the farmers occasionally in the lighter labors of their farms, helped to make hay, mended the fences, took the horses to water, drove the cows from pasture, and cut wood for the winter fire. He laid aside, too, all the dominant dignity and absolute sway with which he lorded it in his little empire, the school, and became wonderfully gentle and ingratiating. He found favor in the eyes of the mothers by petting the children, particularly the youngest; and like the lion bold, which whilom so magnanimously the lamb did hold, he would sit with a child on one knee, and rock a cradle with his foot for whole hours together.

In addition to his other vocations, he was the singing-master of the neighborhood, and picked up many bright shillings by instructing the young folks in psalmody. It was a matter of no little vanity to him on Sundays, to take his station in front of the church gallery, with a band of chosen singers; where, in his own mind, he completely carried away the palm from the parson. Certain it is, his voice resounded far above all the rest of the congregation; and there are peculiar quavers still to be heard in that church, and which may even be heard half a mile off, quite to the opposite side of the millpond, on a still Sunday morning, which are said to be legitimately descended from the nose of Ichabod Crane. Thus, by divers little makeshifts, in that ingenious way which is commonly denominated "by hook and by crook," the worthy pedagogue got on tolerably enough, and was thought, by all who understood nothing of the labor of headwork, to have a wonderfully easy life of it.

The schoolmaster is generally a man of some importance in the female circle of a rural neighborhood; being considered a kind of idle, gentlemanlike personage, of vastly superior taste and accomplishments to the rough country swains, and, indeed, inferior in learning only to the parson. His appearance, therefore, is apt to occasion some little stir at the tea-table of a farmhouse, and the addition of a supernumerary dish of cakes or sweetmeats, or, peradventure, the parade of a silver teapot. Our man of letters, therefore, was peculiarly happy in the smiles of all the country damsels. How he would figure among them in the churchyard, between services on Sundays; gathering grapes for them from the wild vines that overran the surrounding trees; reciting for their amusement all the epitaphs on the tombstones; or sauntering, with a whole bevy of them, along the banks of the adjacent millpond; while the more bashful country bumpkins hung sheepishly back, envying his superior elegance and address.

From his half-itinerant life, also, he was a kind of travelling gazette, carrying the whole budget of local gossip from house to house, so that his appearance was always greeted with satisfaction. He was, moreover, esteemed by the women as a man of great erudition, for he had read several books quite through, and was a perfect master of Cotton Mather's "History of New England Witchcraft," in which, by the way, he most firmly and potently believed.

He was, in fact, an odd mixture of small shrewdness and simple credulity. His appetite for the marvelous, and his powers of digesting it, were equally extraordinary; and both had been increased by his residence in this spell-bound region. No tale was too gross or monstrous for his capacious swallow. It was often his delight, after his school was dismissed in the afternoon, to stretch himself on the rich bed of clover bordering the little brook that whimpered by his schoolhouse, and there con over old Mather's direful tales, until the gathering dusk of evening made the printed page a mere mist before his eyes. Then, as he wended his way by swamp and stream and awful woodland, to the farmhouse where he happened to be quartered, every sound of nature, at that witching hour, fluttered his excited imagination,--the moan of the whip-poor-will from the hillside, the boding cry of the tree toad, that harbinger of storm, the dreary hooting of the screech owl, or the sudden rustling in the thicket of birds frightened from their roost. The fireflies, too, which sparkled most vividly in the darkest places, now and then startled him, as one of uncommon brightness would stream across his path; and if, by chance, a huge blockhead of a beetle came winging his blundering flight against him, the poor varlet was ready to give up the ghost, with the idea that he was struck with a witch's token. His only resource on such occasions, either to drown thought or drive away evil spirits, was to sing psalm tunes and the good people of Sleepy Hollow, as they sat by their doors of an evening, were often filled with awe at hearing his nasal melody, "in linked sweetness long drawn out," floating from the distant hill, or along the dusky road.

Another of his sources of fearful pleasure was to pass long winter evenings with the old Dutch wives, as they sat spinning by the fire, with a row of apples roasting and spluttering along the hearth, and listen to their marvelous tales of ghosts and goblins, and haunted fields, and haunted brooks, and haunted bridges, and haunted houses, and particularly of the headless horseman, or Galloping Hessian of the Hollow, as they sometimes called him. He would delight them equally by his anecdotes of witchcraft, and of the direful omens and portentous sights and sounds in the air, which prevailed in the earlier times of Connecticut; and would frighten them woefully with speculations upon comets and shooting stars; and with the alarming fact that the world did absolutely turn round, and that they were half the time topsy-turvy!

But if there was a pleasure in all this, while snugly cuddling in the chimney corner of a chamber that was all of a ruddy glow from the crackling wood fire, and where, of course, no spectre dared to show its face, it was dearly purchased by the terrors of his subsequent walk homewards. What fearful shapes and shadows beset his path, amidst the dim and ghastly glare of a snowy night!

With what wistful look did he eye every trembling ray of light streaming across the waste fields from some distant window! How often was he appalled by some shrub covered with snow, which, like a sheeted spectre, beset his very path! How often did he shrink with curdling awe at the sound of his own steps on the frosty crust beneath his feet; and dread to look over his shoulder, lest he should behold some uncouth being tramping close behind him! And how often was he thrown into complete dismay by some rushing blast, howling among the trees, in the idea that it was the Galloping Hessian on one of his nightly scourings!

All these, however, were mere terrors of the night, phantoms of the mind that walk in darkness; and though he had seen many spectres in his time, and been more than once beset by Satan in divers shapes, in his lonely perambulations, yet daylight put an end to all these evils; and he would have passed a pleasant life of it, in despite of the Devil and all his works, if his path had not been crossed by a being that causes more perplexity to mortal man than ghosts, goblins, and the whole race of witches put together, and that was--a woman.

Among the musical disciples who assembled, one evening in each week, to receive his instructions in psalmody, was Katrina Van Tassel, the daughter and only child of a substantial Dutch farmer. She was a blooming lass of fresh eighteen; plump as a partridge; ripe and melting and rosy-cheeked as one of her father's peaches, and universally famed, not merely for her beauty, but her vast expectations. She was withal a little of a coquette, as might be perceived even in her dress, which was a mixture of ancient and modern fashions, as most suited to set off her charms. She wore the ornaments of pure yellow gold, which her great-great-grandmother had brought over from Saardam; the tempting stomacher of the olden time, and withal a provokingly short petticoat, to display the prettiest foot and ankle in the country round.

Ichabod Crane had a soft and foolish heart towards the sex; and it is not to be wondered at that so tempting a morsel soon found favor in his eyes, more especially after he had visited her in her paternal mansion. Old Baltus Van Tassel was a perfect picture of a thriving, contented, liberal-hearted farmer. He seldom, it is true, sent either his eyes or his thoughts beyond the boundaries of his own farm; but within those everything was snug, happy and well-conditioned. He was satisfied with his wealth, but not proud of it; and piqued himself upon the hearty abundance, rather than the style in which he lived. His stronghold was situated on the banks of the Hudson, in one of those green, sheltered, fertile nooks in which the Dutch farmers are so fond of nestling. A great elm tree spread its broad branches over it, at the foot of which bubbled up a spring of the softest and sweetest water, in a little well formed of a barrel; and then stole sparkling away through the grass, to a neighboring brook, that babbled along among alders and dwarf willows. Hard by the farmhouse was a vast barn, that might have served for a church; every window and crevice of which seemed bursting forth with the treasures of the farm; the flail was busily resounding within it from morning to night; swallows and martins skimmed twittering about the eaves; and rows of pigeons, some with one eye turned up, as if watching the weather, some with their heads under their wings or buried in their bosoms, and others swelling, and cooing, and bowing about their dames, were enjoying the sunshine on the roof. Sleek unwieldy porkers were grunting in the repose and abundance of their pens, from whence sallied forth, now and then, troops of sucking pigs, as if to snuff the air. A stately squadron of snowy geese were riding in an adjoining pond, convoying whole fleets of ducks; regiments of turkeys were gobbling through the farmyard, and Guinea fowls fretting about it, like ill-tempered housewives, with their peevish, discontented cry. Before the barn door strutted the gallant cock, that pattern of a husband, a warrior and a fine gentleman, clapping his burnished wings and crowing in the pride and gladness of his heart,--sometimes tearing up the earth with his feet, and then generously calling his ever-hungry family of wives and children to enjoy the rich morsel which he had discovered.

The pedagogue's mouth watered as he looked upon this sumptuous promise of luxurious winter fare. In his devouring mind's eye, he pictured to himself every roasting-pig running about with a pudding in his belly, and an apple in his mouth; the pigeons were snugly put to bed in a comfortable pie, and tucked in with a coverlet of crust; the geese were swimming in their own gravy; and the ducks pairing cozily in dishes, like snug married couples, with a decent competency of onion sauce. In the porkers he saw carved out the future sleek side of bacon, and juicy relishing ham; not a turkey but he beheld daintily trussed up, with its gizzard under its wing, and, peradventure, a necklace of savory sausages; and even bright chanticleer himself lay sprawling on his back, in a side dish, with uplifted claws, as if craving that quarter which his chivalrous spirit disdained to ask while living.

As the enraptured Ichabod fancied all this, and as he rolled his great green eyes over the fat meadow lands, the rich fields of wheat, of rye, of buckwheat, and Indian corn, and the orchards burdened with ruddy fruit, which surrounded the warm tenement of Van Tassel, his heart yearned after the damsel who was to inherit these domains, and his imagination expanded with the idea, how they might be readily turned into cash, and the money invested in immense tracts of wild land, and shingle palaces in the wilderness. Nay, his busy fancy already realized his hopes, and presented to him the blooming Katrina, with a whole family of children, mounted on the top of a wagon loaded with household trumpery, with pots and kettles dangling beneath; and he beheld himself bestriding a pacing mare, with a colt at her heels, setting out for Kentucky, Tennessee,--or the Lord knows where!

When he entered the house, the conquest of his heart was complete. It was one of those spacious farmhouses, with high-ridged but lowly sloping roofs, built in the style handed down from the first Dutch settlers; the low projecting eaves forming a piazza along the front, capable of being closed up in bad weather. Under this were hung flails, harness, various utensils of husbandry, and nets for fishing in the neighboring river. Benches were built along the sides for summer use; and a great spinning-wheel at one end, and a churn at the other, showed the various uses to which this important porch might be devoted. From this piazza the wondering Ichabod entered the hall, which formed the centre of the mansion, and the place of usual residence. Here rows of resplendent pewter, ranged on a long dresser, dazzled his eyes. In one corner stood a huge bag of wool, ready to be spun; in another, a quantity of linsey-woolsey just from the loom; ears of Indian corn, and strings of dried apples and peaches, hung in gay festoons along the walls, mingled with the gaud of red peppers; and a door left ajar gave him a peep into the best parlor, where the claw-footed chairs and dark mahogany tables shone like mirrors; andirons, with their accompanying shovel and tongs, glistened from their covert of asparagus tops; mock-oranges and conch-shells decorated the mantelpiece; strings of various-colored birds eggs were suspended above it; a great ostrich egg was hung from the centre of the room, and a corner cupboard, knowingly left open, displayed immense treasures of old silver and well-mended china.

From the moment Ichabod laid his eyes upon these regions of delight, the peace of his mind was at an end, and his only study was how to gain the affections of the peerless daughter of Van Tassel. In this enterprise, however, he had more real difficulties than generally fell to the lot of a knight-errant of yore, who seldom had anything but giants, enchanters, fiery dragons, and such like easily conquered adversaries, to contend with and had to make his way merely through gates of iron and brass, and walls of adamant to the castle keep, where the lady of his heart was confined; all which he achieved as easily as a man would carve his way to the centre of a Christmas pie; and then the lady gave him her hand as a matter of course. Ichabod, on the contrary, had to win his way to the heart of a country coquette, beset with a labyrinth of whims and caprices, which were forever presenting new difficulties and impediments; and he had to encounter a host of fearful adversaries of real flesh and blood, the numerous rustic admirers, who beset every portal to her heart, keeping a watchful and angry eye upon each other, but ready to fly out in the common cause against any new competitor.

Among these, the most formidable was a burly, roaring, roistering blade, of the name of Abraham, or, according to the Dutch abbreviation, Brom Van Brunt, the hero of the country round, which rang with his feats of strength and hardihood. He was broad-shouldered and double-jointed, with short curly black hair, and a bluff but not unpleasant countenance, having a mingled air of fun and arrogance. From his Herculean frame and great powers of limb he had received the nickname of BROM BONES, by which he was universally known. He was famed for great knowledge and skill in horsemanship, being as dexterous on horseback as a Tartar. He was foremost at all races and cock fights;

and, with the ascendancy which bodily strength always acquires in rustic life, was the umpire in all disputes, setting his hat on one side, and giving his decisions with an air and tone that admitted of no gainsay or appeal. He was always ready for either a fight or a frolic; but had more mischief than ill-will in his composition; and with all his overbearing roughness, there was a strong dash of waggish good humor at bottom. He had three or four boon companions, who regarded him as their model, and at the head of whom he scoured the country, attending every scene of feud or merriment for miles round. In cold weather he was distinguished by a fur cap, surmounted with a flaunting fox's tail; and when the folks at a country gathering descried this well-known crest at a distance, whisking about among a squad of hard riders, they always stood by for a squall. Sometimes his crew would be heard dashing along past the farmhouses at midnight, with whoop and halloo, like a troop of Don Cossacks; and the old dames, startled out of their sleep, would listen for a moment till the hurry-scurry had clattered by, and then exclaim, "Ay, there goes Brom Bones and his gang!" The neighbors looked upon him with a mixture of awe, admiration, and good-will; and, when any madcap prank or rustic brawl occurred in the vicinity, always shook their heads, and warranted Brom Bones was at the bottom of it.

This rantipole hero had for some time singled out the blooming Katrina for the object of his uncouth gallantries, and though his amorous toyings were something like the gentle caresses and endearments of a bear, yet it was whispered that she did not altogether discourage his hopes. Certain it is, his advances were signals for rival candidates to retire, who felt no inclination to cross a lion in his amours; insomuch, that when his horse was seen tied to Van Tassel's paling, on a Sunday night, a sure sign that his master was courting, or, as it is termed, "sparking," within, all other suitors passed by in despair, and carried the war into other quarters.

Such was the formidable rival with whom Ichabod Crane had to contend, and, considering all things, a stouter man than he would have shrunk from the competition, and a wiser man would have despaired. He had, however, a happy mixture of pliability and perseverance in his nature; he was in form and spirit like a supple-jack--yielding, but tough; though he bent, he never broke; and though he bowed beneath the slightest pressure, yet, the moment it was away--jerk!--he was as erect, and carried his head as high as ever.

To have taken the field openly against his rival would have been madness; for he was not a man to be thwarted in his amours, any more than that stormy lover, Achilles. Ichabod, therefore, made his advances in a quiet and gently insinuating manner. Under cover of his character of singing-master, he made frequent visits at the farmhouse; not that he had anything to apprehend from the meddlesome interference of parents, which is so often a stumbling-block in the path of lovers. Balt Van Tassel was an easy indulgent soul; he loved his daughter better even than his pipe, and, like a reasonable man and an excellent father, let her have her way in everything. His notable little wife, too, had enough to do to attend to her housekeeping and manage her poultry; for, as she sagely observed, ducks and geese are foolish things, and must be looked after, but girls can take care of themselves. Thus, while the busy dame bustled about the house, or plied her spinning-wheel at one end of the piazza, honest Balt would sit smoking his evening pipe at the other, watching the achievements of a little wooden warrior, who, armed with a sword in each hand, was most valiantly fighting the wind on the pinnacle of the barn. In the mean time, Ichabod would carry on his suit with the daughter by the side of the spring under the great elm, or sauntering along in the twilight, that hour so favorable to the lover's eloquence.

I profess not to know how women's hearts are wooed and won. To me they have always been matters of riddle and admiration. Some seem to have but one vulnerable point, or door of access; while others have a thousand avenues, and may be captured in a thousand different ways. It is a great triumph of skill to gain the former, but a still greater proof of generalship to maintain possession of the latter, for man must battle for his fortress at every door and window. He who wins a thousand common hearts is therefore entitled to some renown; but he who keeps undisputed sway over the heart of a coquette is indeed a hero. Certain it is, this was not the case with the redoubtable Brom Bones; and from the moment Ichabod Crane made his advances, the interests of the former evidently declined: his horse was no longer seen tied to the palings on Sunday nights, and a deadly feud gradually arose between him and the preceptor of Sleepy Hollow.

Brom, who had a degree of rough chivalry in his nature, would fain have carried matters to open warfare and have settled their pretensions to the lady, according to the mode of those most concise and simple reasoners, the knights-errant of yore,--by single combat; but Ichabod was too conscious of the superior might of his adversary to enter the lists against him; he had overheard a boast of Bones, that he would "double the schoolmaster up, and lay him on a shelf of his own schoolhouse;" and he was too wary to give him an opportunity. There was something extremely provoking in this obstinately pacific system; it left Brom no alternative but to draw upon the funds of rustic waggery in his disposition, and to play off boorish practical jokes upon his rival. Ichabod became the object of whimsical persecution to Bones and his gang of rough riders. They harried his hitherto peaceful domains; smoked out his singing school by stopping up the chimney; broke into the schoolhouse at night, in spite of its formidable fastenings of with and window stakes, and turned everything topsy-turvy, so that the poor schoolmaster began to think all the witches in the country held their meetings there. But what was still more annoying, Brom took all opportunities of turning him into ridicule in presence of his mistress, and had a scoundrel dog whom he taught to whine in the most ludicrous manner, and introduced as a rival of Ichabod's, to instruct her in psalmody.

In this way matters went on for some time, without producing any material effect on the relative situations of the contending powers. On a fine autumnal afternoon, Ichabod, in pensive mood, sat enthroned on the lofty stool from whence he usually watched all the concerns of his little literary realm. In his hand he swayed a ferule, that sceptre of despotic power; the birch of justice reposed on three nails behind the throne, a constant terror to evil doers, while on the desk before him might be seen sundry contraband articles and prohibited weapons, detected upon the persons of idle urchins, such as half-munched apples, popguns, whirligigs, fly-cages, and whole legions of rampant little paper gamecocks. Apparently there had been some appalling act of justice recently inflicted, for his scholars were all busily intent upon their books, or slyly whispering behind them with one eye kept upon the master; and a kind of buzzing stillness reigned throughout the schoolroom. It was suddenly interrupted by the appearance of a negro in tow-cloth jacket and trowsers, a round-crowned fragment of a hat, like the cap of Mercury, and mounted on the back of a ragged, wild, half-broken colt, which he managed with a rope by way of halter. He came clattering up to the school door with an invitation to Ichabod to attend a merry-making or "quilting frolic," to be held that evening at Mynheer Van Tassel's; and having delivered his message with that air of importance, and effort at fine language, which a negro is apt to display on petty embassies of the kind, he dashed over the brook, and was seen scampering away up the hollow, full of the importance and hurry of his mission.

All was now bustle and hubbub in the late quiet schoolroom. The scholars were hurried through their lessons without stopping at trifles; those who were nimble skipped over half with impunity, and those who were tardy had a smart application now and then in the rear, to quicken their speed or help them over a tall word. Books were flung aside without being put away on the shelves, inkstands were overturned, benches thrown down, and the whole school was turned loose an hour before the usual time, bursting forth like a legion of young imps, yelping and racketing about the green in joy at their early emancipation.

The gallant Ichabod now spent at least an extra half hour at his toilet, brushing and furbishing up his best, and indeed only suit of rusty black, and arranging his locks by a bit of broken looking-glass that hung up in the schoolhouse. That he might make his appearance before his mistress in the true style of a cavalier, he borrowed a horse from the farmer with whom he was domiciliated, a choleric old Dutchman of the name of Hans Van Ripper, and, thus gallantly mounted, issued forth like a knight-errant in quest of adventures. But it is meet I should, in the true spirit of romantic story, give some account of the looks and equipments of my hero and his steed. The animal he bestrode was a broken-down plow-horse, that had outlived almost everything but its viciousness. He was gaunt and shagged, with a ewe neck, and a head like a hammer; his rusty mane and tail were tangled and knotted with burs; one eye had lost its pupil, and was glaring and spectral, but the other had the gleam of a genuine devil in it. Still he must have had fire and mettle in his day, if we may judge from the name he bore of Gunpowder. He had, in fact, been a favorite steed of his master's, the choleric Van Ripper, who was a furious rider, and had infused, very probably, some of his own spirit into the animal; for, old and broken-down as he looked, there was more of the lurking devil in him than in any young filly in the country.

Ichabod was a suitable figure for such a steed. He rode with short stirrups, which brought his knees nearly up to the pommel of the saddle; his sharp elbows stuck out like grasshoppers'; he carried his whip perpendicularly in his hand, like a sceptre, and as his horse jogged on, the motion of his arms was not unlike the flapping of a pair of wings. A small wool hat rested on the top of his nose, for so his scanty strip of forehead might be called, and the skirts of his black coat fluttered out almost to the horses tail. Such was the appearance of Ichabod and his steed as they shambled out of the gate of Hans Van Ripper, and it was altogether such an apparition as is seldom to be met with in broad daylight.

It was, as I have said, a fine autumnal day; the sky was clear and serene, and nature wore that rich and golden livery which we always associate with the idea of abundance. The forests had put on their sober brown and yellow, while some trees of the tenderer kind had been nipped by the frosts into brilliant dyes of orange, purple, and scarlet. Streaming files of wild ducks began to make their appearance high in the air; the bark of the squirrel might be heard from the groves of beech and hickory-nuts, and the pensive whistle of the quail at intervals from the neighboring stubble field.

The small birds were taking their farewell banquets. In the fullness of their revelry, they fluttered, chirping and frolicking from bush to bush, and tree to tree, capricious from the very profusion and variety around them. There was the honest cock robin, the favorite game of stripling sportsmen, with its loud querulous note; and the twittering blackbirds flying in sable clouds; and the golden-winged woodpecker with his crimson crest, his broad black gorget, and splendid plumage; and the cedar bird, with its red-tipt wings and yellow-tipt tail and its little monteiro cap of feathers; and the blue jay, that noisy coxcomb, in his gay light blue coat and white underclothes, screaming and chattering, nodding and bobbing and bowing, and pretending to be on good terms with every songster of the grove.

As Ichabod jogged slowly on his way, his eye, ever open to every symptom of culinary abundance, ranged with delight over the treasures of jolly autumn. On all sides he beheld vast store of apples; some hanging in oppressive opulence on the trees; some gathered into baskets and barrels for the market; others heaped up in rich piles for the cider-press. Farther on he beheld great fields of Indian corn, with its golden ears peeping from their leafy coverts, and holding out the promise of cakes and hasty-pudding; and the yellow pumpkins lying beneath them, turning up their fair round bellies to the sun, and giving ample prospects of the most luxurious of pies; and anon he passed the fragrant buckwheat fields breathing the odor of the beehive, and as he beheld them, soft anticipations stole over his mind of dainty slapjacks, well buttered, and garnished with honey or treacle, by the delicate little dimpled hand of Katrina Van Tassel.

Thus feeding his mind with many sweet thoughts and "sugared suppositions," he journeyed along the sides of a range of hills which look out upon some of the goodliest scenes of the mighty Hudson. The sun gradually wheeled his broad disk down in the west. The wide bosom of the Tappan Zee lay motionless and glassy, excepting that here and there a gentle undulation waved and prolonged the blue shadow of the distant mountain. A few amber clouds floated in the sky, without a breath of air to move them. The horizon was of a fine golden tint, changing gradually into a pure apple green, and from that into the deep blue of the mid-heaven. A slanting ray lingered on the woody crests of the precipices that overhung some parts of the river, giving greater depth to the dark gray and purple of their rocky sides. A sloop was loitering in the distance, dropping slowly down with the tide, her sail hanging uselessly against the mast; and as the reflection of the sky gleamed along the still water, it seemed as if the vessel was suspended in the air.

It was toward evening that Ichabod arrived at the castle of the Heer Van Tassel, which he found thronged with the pride and flower of the adjacent country. Old farmers, a spare leathern-faced race, in homespun coats and breeches, blue stockings, huge shoes, and magnificent pewter buckles. Their brisk, withered little dames, in close-crimped caps, long-waisted short gowns, homespun petticoats, with scissors and pincushions, and gay calico pockets hanging on the outside. Buxom lasses, almost as antiquated as their mothers, excepting where a straw hat, a fine ribbon, or perhaps a white frock, gave symptoms of city innovation. The sons, in short square-skirted coats, with rows of stupendous brass buttons, and their hair generally queued in the fashion of the times, especially if they could procure an eel-skin for the purpose, it being esteemed throughout the country as a potent nourisher and strengthener of the hair.

Brom Bones, however, was the hero of the scene, having come to the gathering on his favorite steed Daredevil, a creature, like himself, full of mettle and mischief, and which no one but himself could manage. He was, in fact, noted for preferring vicious animals, given to all kinds of tricks which kept the rider in constant risk of his neck, for he held a tractable, well-broken horse as unworthy of a lad of spirit.

Fain would I pause to dwell upon the world of charms that burst upon the enraptured gaze of my hero, as he entered the state parlor of Van Tassel's mansion. Not those of the bevy of buxom lasses, with their luxurious display of red and white; but the ample charms of a genuine Dutch country tea-table, in the sumptuous time of autumn. Such heaped up platters of cakes of various and almost indescribable kinds, known only to experienced Dutch housewives! There was the doughty doughnut, the tender olykoek, and the crisp and crumbling cruller; sweet cakes and short cakes, ginger cakes and honey cakes, and the whole family of cakes. And then there were apple pies, and peach pies, and pumpkin pies; besides slices of ham and smoked beef; and moreover delectable dishes of preserved plums, and peaches, and pears, and quinces; not to mention broiled shad and roasted chickens; together with bowls of milk and cream, all mingled higgledy-piggledy, pretty much as I have enumerated them, with the motherly teapot sending up its clouds of vapor from the midst--Heaven bless the mark! I want breath and time to discuss this banquet as it deserves, and am too eager to get on with my story. Happily, Ichabod Crane was not in so great a hurry as his historian, but did ample justice to every dainty.

He was a kind and thankful creature, whose heart dilated in proportion as his skin was filled with good cheer, and whose spirits rose with eating, as some men's do with drink. He could not help, too, rolling his large eyes round him as he ate, and chuckling with the possibility that he might one day be lord of all this scene of almost unimaginable luxury and splendor. Then, he thought, how soon he'd turn his back upon the old schoolhouse; snap his fingers in the face of Hans Van Ripper, and every other patron, and kick any itinerant pedagogue out of doors that should dare to call him comrade!

Old Baltus Van Tassel moved about among his guests with a face dilated with content and good humor, round and jolly as the harvest moon. His hospitable attentions were brief, but expressive, being confined to a shake of the hand, a slap on the shoulder, a loud laugh, and a pressing invitation to "fall to, and help themselves."

And now the sound of the music from the common room, or hall, summoned to the dance. The musician was an old gray-headed negro, who had been the itinerant orchestra of the neighborhood for more than half a century. His instrument was as old and battered as himself. The greater part of the time he scraped on two or three strings, accompanying every movement of the bow with a motion of the head; bowing almost to the ground, and stamping with his foot whenever a fresh couple were to start.

Ichabod prided himself upon his dancing as much as upon his vocal powers. Not a limb, not a fibre about him was idle; and to have seen his loosely hung frame in full motion, and clattering about the room, you would have thought St. Vitus himself, that blessed patron of the dance, was figuring before you in person. He was the admiration of all the negroes; who, having gathered, of all ages and sizes, from the farm and the neighborhood, stood forming a pyramid of shining black faces at every door and window, gazing with delight at the scene, rolling their white eyeballs, and showing grinning rows of ivory from ear to ear. How could the flogger of urchins be otherwise than animated and joyous? The lady of his heart was his partner in the dance, and smiling graciously in reply to all his amorous oglings; while Brom Bones, sorely smitten with love and jealousy, sat brooding by himself in one corner.

When the dance was at an end, Ichabod was attracted to a knot of the sager folks, who, with Old Van Tassel, sat smoking at one end of the piazza, gossiping over former times, and drawing out long stories about the war.

This neighborhood, at the time of which I am speaking, was one of those highly favored places which abound with chronicle and great men. The British and American line had run near it during the war; it had, therefore, been the scene of marauding and infested with refugees, cowboys, and all kinds of border chivalry. Just sufficient time had elapsed to enable each storyteller to dress up his tale with a little becoming fiction, and, in the indistinctness of his recollection, to make himself the hero of every exploit.

There was the story of Doffue Martling, a large blue-bearded Dutchman, who had nearly taken a British frigate with an old iron nine-pounder from a mud breastwork, only that his gun burst at the sixth discharge. And there was an old gentleman who shall be nameless, being too rich a mynheer to be lightly mentioned, who, in the battle of White Plains, being an excellent master of defense, parried a musket-ball with a small sword, insomuch that he absolutely felt it whiz round the blade, and glance off at the hilt; in proof of which he was ready at any time to show the sword, with the hilt a little bent. There were several more that had been equally great in the field, not one of whom but was persuaded that he had a considerable hand in bringing the war to a happy termination.

But all these were nothing to the tales of ghosts and apparitions that succeeded. The neighborhood is rich in legendary treasures of the kind. Local tales and superstitions thrive best in these sheltered, long-settled retreats; but are trampled under foot by the shifting throng that forms the population of most of our country places. Besides, there is no encouragement for ghosts in most of our villages, for they have scarcely had time to finish their first nap and turn themselves in their graves, before their surviving friends have travelled away from the neighborhood; so that when they turn out at night to walk their rounds, they have no acquaintance left to call upon. This is perhaps the reason why we so seldom hear of ghosts except in our long-established Dutch communities.

The immediate cause, however, of the prevalence of supernatural stories in these parts, was doubtless owing to the vicinity of Sleepy Hollow. There was a contagion in the very air that blew from that haunted region; it breathed forth an atmosphere of dreams and fancies infecting all the land. Several of the Sleepy Hollow people were present at Van Tassel's, and, as usual, were doling out their wild and wonderful legends. Many dismal tales were told about funeral trains, and mourning cries and wailings heard and seen about the great tree where the unfortunate Major André was taken, and which stood in the neighborhood. Some mention was made also of the woman in white, that haunted the dark glen at Raven Rock, and was often heard to shriek on winter nights before a storm, having perished there in the snow. The chief part of the stories, however, turned upon the favorite spectre of Sleepy Hollow, the Headless Horseman, who had been heard several times of late, patrolling the country; and, it was said, tethered his horse nightly among the graves in the churchyard.

The sequestered situation of this church seems always to have made it a favorite haunt of troubled spirits. It stands on a knoll, surrounded by locust-trees and lofty elms, from among which its decent, whitewashed walls shine modestly forth, like Christian purity beaming through the shades of retirement. A gentle slope descends from it to a silver sheet of water, bordered by high trees, between which, peeps may be caught at the blue hills of the Hudson. To look upon its grass-grown yard, where the sunbeams seem to sleep so quietly, one would think that there at least the dead might rest in peace. On one side of the church extends a wide woody dell, along which raves a large brook among broken rocks and trunks of fallen trees. Over a deep black part of the stream, not far from the church, was formerly thrown a wooden bridge; the road that led to it, and the bridge itself, were thickly shaded by overhanging trees, which cast a gloom about it, even in the daytime; but occasioned a fearful darkness at night. Such was one of the favorite haunts of the Headless Horseman, and the place where he was most frequently encountered. The tale was told of old Brouwer, a most heretical disbeliever in ghosts, how he met the Horseman returning from his foray into Sleepy Hollow, and was obliged to get up behind him; how they galloped over bush and brake, over hill and swamp, until they reached the bridge; when the Horseman suddenly turned into a skeleton, threw old Brouwer into the brook, and sprang away over the tree-tops with a clap of thunder.

This story was immediately matched by a thrice marvelous adventure of Brom Bones, who made light of the Galloping Hessian as an arrant jockey. He affirmed that on returning one night from the neighboring village of Sing Sing, he had been overtaken by this midnight trooper; that he had offered to race with him for a bowl of punch, and should have won it too, for Daredevil beat the goblin horse all hollow, but just as they came to the church bridge, the Hessian bolted, and vanished in a flash of fire.

All these tales, told in that drowsy undertone with which men talk in the dark, the countenances of the listeners only now and then receiving a casual gleam from the glare of a pipe, sank deep in the mind of Ichabod. He repaid them in kind with large extracts from his invaluable author, Cotton Mather, and added many marvelous events that had taken place in his native State of Connecticut, and fearful sights which he had seen in his nightly walks about Sleepy Hollow.

The revel now gradually broke up. The old farmers gathered together their families in their wagons, and were heard for some time rattling along the hollow roads, and over the distant hills. Some of the damsels mounted on pillions behind their favorite swains, and their light-hearted laughter, mingling with the clatter of hoofs, echoed along the silent woodlands, sounding fainter and fainter, until they gradually died away,--and the late scene of noise and frolic was all silent and deserted. Ichabod only lingered behind, according to the custom of country lovers, to have a tête-à-tête with the heiress; fully convinced that he was now on the high road to success. What passed at this interview I will not pretend to say, for in fact I do not know. Something, however, I fear me, must have gone wrong, for he certainly sallied forth, after no very great interval, with an air quite desolate and chap-fallen. Oh, these women! these women! Could that girl have been playing off any of her coquettish tricks? Was her encouragement of the poor pedagogue all a mere sham to secure her conquest of his rival? Heaven only knows, not I! Let it suffice to say, Ichabod stole forth with the air of one who had been sacking a henroost, rather than a fair lady's heart. Without looking to the right or left to notice the scene of rural wealth, on which he had so often gloated, he went straight to the stable, and with several hearty cuffs and kicks roused his steed most uncourteously from the comfortable quarters in which he was soundly sleeping, dreaming of mountains of corn and oats, and whole valleys of timothy and clover.

It was the very witching time of night that Ichabod, heavy-hearted and crestfallen, pursued his travels homewards, along the sides of the lofty hills which rise above Tarry Town, and which he had traversed so cheerily in the afternoon. The hour was as dismal as himself. Far below him the Tappan Zee spread its dusky and indistinct waste of waters, with here and there the tall mast of a sloop, riding quietly at anchor under the land. In the dead hush of midnight, he could even hear the barking of the watchdog from the opposite shore of the Hudson; but it was so vague and faint as only to give an idea of his distance from this faithful companion of man. Now and then, too, the long-drawn crowing of a cock, accidentally awakened, would sound far, far off, from some farmhouse away among the hills--but it was like a dreaming sound in his ear. No signs of life occurred near him, but occasionally the melancholy chirp of a cricket, or perhaps the guttural twang of a bullfrog from a neighboring marsh, as if sleeping uncomfortably and turning suddenly in his bed.

All the stories of ghosts and goblins that he had heard in the afternoon now came crowding upon his recollection. The night grew darker and darker; the stars seemed to sink deeper in the sky, and driving clouds occasionally hid them from his sight. He had never felt so lonely and dismal. He was, moreover, approaching the very place where many of the scenes of the ghost stories had been laid. In the centre of the road stood an enormous tulip-tree, which towered like a giant above all the other trees of the neighborhood, and formed a kind of landmark. Its limbs were gnarled and fantastic, large enough to form trunks for ordinary trees, twisting down almost to the earth, and rising again into the air. It was connected with the tragical story of the unfortunate André, who had been taken prisoner hard by; and was universally known by the name of Major André's tree. The common people regarded it with a mixture of respect and superstition, partly out of sympathy for the fate of its ill-starred namesake, and partly from the tales of strange sights, and doleful lamentations, told concerning it.

As Ichabod approached this fearful tree, he began to whistle; he thought his whistle was answered; it was but a blast sweeping sharply through the dry branches. As he approached a little nearer, he thought he saw something white, hanging in the midst of the tree: he paused and ceased whistling but, on looking more narrowly, perceived that it was a place where the tree had been scathed by lightning, and the white wood laid bare. Suddenly he heard a groan--his teeth chattered, and his knees smote against the saddle: it was but the rubbing of one huge bough upon another, as they were swayed about by the breeze. He passed the tree in safety, but new perils lay before him.

About two hundred yards from the tree, a small brook crossed the road, and ran into a marshy and thickly-wooded glen, known by the name of Wiley's Swamp. A few rough logs, laid side by side, served for a bridge over this stream. On that side of the road where the brook entered the wood, a group of oaks and chestnuts, matted thick with wild grape-vines, threw a cavernous gloom over it. To pass this bridge was the severest trial. It was at this identical spot that the unfortunate André was captured, and under the covert of those chestnuts and vines were the sturdy yeomen concealed who surprised him. This has ever since been considered a haunted stream, and fearful are the feelings of the schoolboy who has to pass it alone after dark.

As he approached the stream, his heart began to thump; he summoned up, however, all his resolution, gave his horse half a score of kicks in the ribs, and attempted to dash briskly across the bridge; but instead of starting forward, the perverse old animal made a lateral movement, and ran broadside against the fence. Ichabod, whose fears increased with the delay, jerked the reins on the other side, and kicked lustily with the contrary foot: it was all in vain; his steed started, it is true, but it was only to plunge to the opposite side of the road into a thicket of brambles and alder bushes. The schoolmaster now bestowed both whip and heel upon the starveling ribs of old Gunpowder, who dashed forward, snuffling and snorting, but came to a stand just by the bridge, with a suddenness that had nearly sent his rider sprawling over his head. Just at this moment a plashy tramp by the side of the bridge caught the sensitive ear of Ichabod. In the dark shadow of the grove, on the margin of the brook, he beheld something huge, misshapen and towering. It stirred not, but seemed gathered up in the gloom, like some gigantic monster ready to spring upon the traveler.

The hair of the affrighted pedagogue rose upon his head with terror. What was to be done? To turn and fly was now too late; and besides, what chance was there of escaping ghost or goblin, if such it was, which could ride upon the wings of the wind? Summoning up, therefore, a show of courage, he demanded in stammering accents, "Who are you?" He received no reply. He repeated his demand in a still more agitated voice. Still there was no answer. Once more he cudgeled the sides of the inflexible Gunpowder, and, shutting his eyes, broke forth with involuntary fervor into a psalm tune. Just then the shadowy object of alarm put itself in motion, and with a scramble and a bound stood at once in the middle of the road. Though the night was dark and dismal, yet the form of the unknown might now in some degree be ascertained. He appeared to be a horseman of large dimensions, and mounted on a black horse of powerful frame. He made no offer of molestation or sociability, but kept aloof on one side of the road, jogging along on the blind side of old Gunpowder, who had now got over his fright and waywardness.

Ichabod, who had no relish for this strange midnight companion, and bethought himself of the adventure of Brom Bones with the Galloping Hessian, now quickened his steed in hopes of leaving him behind. The stranger, however, quickened his horse to an equal pace. Ichabod pulled up, and fell into a walk, thinking to lag behind,--the other did the same. His heart began to sink within him; he endeavored to resume his psalm tune, but his parched tongue clove to the roof of his mouth, and he could not utter a stave. There was something in the moody and dogged silence of this pertinacious companion that was mysterious and appalling. It was soon fearfully accounted for. On mounting a rising ground, which brought the figure of his fellow-traveler in relief against the sky, gigantic in height, and muffled in a cloak, Ichabod was horror-struck on perceiving that he was headless!--but his horror was still more increased on observing that the head, which should have rested on his shoulders, was carried before him on the pommel of his saddle! His terror rose to desperation; he rained a shower of kicks and blows upon Gunpowder, hoping by a sudden movement to give his companion the slip; but the spectre started full jump with him. Away, then, they dashed through thick and thin; stones flying and sparks flashing at every bound. Ichabod's flimsy garments fluttered in the air, as he stretched his long lank body away over his horse's head, in the eagerness of his flight.

They had now reached the road which turns off to Sleepy Hollow; but Gunpowder, who seemed possessed with a demon, instead of keeping up it, made an opposite turn, and plunged headlong downhill to the left. This road leads through a sandy hollow shaded by trees for about a quarter of a mile, where it crosses the bridge famous in goblin story; and just beyond swells the green knoll on which stands the whitewashed church.

As yet the panic of the steed had given his unskillful rider an apparent advantage in the chase, but just as he had got half way through the hollow, the girths of the saddle gave way, and he felt it slipping from under him. He seized it by the pommel, and endeavored to hold it firm, but in vain; and had just time to save himself by clasping old Gunpowder round the neck, when the saddle fell to the earth, and he heard it trampled under foot by his pursuer. For a moment the terror of Hans Van Ripper's wrath passed across his mind,--for it was his Sunday saddle; but this was no time for petty fears; the goblin was hard on his haunches; and (unskillful rider that he was!) he had much ado to maintain his seat; sometimes slipping on one side, sometimes on another, and sometimes jolted on the high ridge of his horse's backbone, with a violence that he verily feared would cleave him asunder.

An opening in the trees now cheered him with the hopes that the church bridge was at hand. The wavering reflection of a silver star in the bosom of the brook told him that he was not mistaken. He saw the walls of the church dimly glaring under the trees beyond. He recollected the place where Brom Bones's ghostly competitor had disappeared. "If I can but reach that bridge," thought Ichabod, "I am safe." Just then he heard the black steed panting and blowing close behind him; he even fancied that he felt his hot breath. Another convulsive kick in the ribs, and old Gunpowder sprang upon the bridge; he thundered over the resounding planks; he gained the opposite side; and now Ichabod cast a look behind to see if his pursuer should vanish, according to rule, in a flash of fire and brimstone. Just then he saw the goblin rising in his stirrups, and in the very act of hurling his head at him. Ichabod endeavored to dodge the horrible missile, but too late. It encountered his cranium with a tremendous crash,--he was tumbled headlong into the dust, and Gunpowder, the black steed, and the goblin rider, passed by like a whirlwind.

The next morning the old horse was found without his saddle, and with the bridle under his feet, soberly cropping the grass at his master's gate. Ichabod did not make his appearance at breakfast; dinner-hour came, but no Ichabod. The boys assembled at the schoolhouse, and strolled idly about the banks of the brook; but no schoolmaster. Hans Van Ripper now began to feel some uneasiness about the fate of poor Ichabod, and his saddle. An inquiry was set on foot, and after diligent investigation they came upon his traces. In one part of the road leading to the church was found the saddle trampled in the dirt; the tracks of horses' hoofs deeply dented in the road, and evidently at furious speed, were traced to the bridge, beyond which, on the bank of a broad part of the brook, where the water ran deep and black, was found the hat of the unfortunate Ichabod, and close beside it a shattered pumpkin.

The brook was searched, but the body of the schoolmaster was not to be discovered. Hans Van Ripper as executor of his estate, examined the bundle which contained all his worldly effects. They consisted of two shirts and a half; two stocks for the neck; a pair or two of worsted stockings; an old pair of corduroy small-clothes; a rusty razor; a book of psalm tunes full of dog's-ears; and a broken pitch-pipe. As to the books and furniture of the schoolhouse, they belonged to the community, excepting Cotton Mather's "History of Witchcraft," a "New England Almanac," and a book of dreams and fortune-telling; in which last was a sheet of foolscap much scribbled and blotted in several fruitless attempts to make a copy of verses in honor of the heiress of Van Tassel. These magic books and the poetic scrawl were forthwith consigned to the flames by Hans Van Ripper; who, from that time forward, determined to send his children no more to school, observing that he never knew any good come of this same reading and writing. Whatever money the schoolmaster possessed, and he had received his quarter's pay but a day or two before, he must have had about his person at the time of his disappearance.

The mysterious event caused much speculation at the church on the following Sunday. Knots of gazers and gossips were collected in the churchyard, at the bridge, and at the spot where the hat and pumpkin had been found. The stories of Brouwer, of Bones, and a whole budget of others were called to mind; and when they had diligently considered them all, and compared them with the symptoms of the present case, they shook their heads, and came to the conclusion that Ichabod had been carried off by the Galloping Hessian. As he was a bachelor, and in nobody's debt, nobody troubled his head any more about him; the school was removed to a different quarter of the hollow, and another pedagogue reigned in his stead.

It is true, an old farmer, who had been down to New York on a visit several years after, and from whom this account of the ghostly adventure was received, brought home the intelligence that Ichabod Crane was still alive; that he had left the neighborhood partly through fear of the goblin and Hans Van Ripper, and partly in mortification at having been suddenly dismissed by the heiress; that he had changed his quarters to a distant part of the country; had kept school and studied law at the same time; had been admitted to the bar; turned politician; electioneered; written for the newspapers; and finally had been made a justice of the Ten Pound Court. Brom Bones, too, who, shortly after his rival's disappearance conducted the blooming Katrina in triumph to the altar, was observed to look exceedingly knowing whenever the story of Ichabod was related, and always burst into a hearty laugh at the mention of the pumpkin; which led some to suspect that he knew more about the matter than he chose to tell.

The old country wives, however, who are the best judges of these matters, maintain to this day that Ichabod was spirited away by supernatural means; and it is a favorite story often told about the neighborhood round the winter evening fire. The bridge became more than ever an object of superstitious awe; and that may be the reason why the road has been altered of late years, so as to approach the church by the border of the millpond. The schoolhouse being deserted soon fell to decay, and was reported to be haunted by the ghost of the unfortunate pedagogue and the plowboy, loitering homeward of a still summer evening, has often fancied his voice at a distance, chanting a melancholy psalm tune among the tranquil solitudes of Sleepy Hollow.

POSTSCRIPT.

FOUND IN THE HANDWRITING OF MR. KNICKERBOCKER.

The preceding tale is given almost in the precise words in which I heard it related at a Corporation meeting at the ancient city of Manhattoes, at which were present many of its sagest and most illustrious burghers. The narrator was a pleasant, shabby, gentlemanly old fellow, in pepper-and-salt clothes, with a sadly humourous face, and one whom I strongly suspected of being poor--he made such efforts to be entertaining. When his story was concluded, there was much laughter and approbation, particularly from two or three deputy aldermen, who had been asleep the greater part of the time. There was, however, one tall, dry-looking old gentleman, with beetling eyebrows, who maintained a grave and rather severe face throughout, now and then folding his arms, inclining his head, and looking down upon the floor, as if turning a doubt over in his mind. He was one of your wary men, who never laugh but upon good grounds--when they have reason and law on their side. When the mirth of the rest of the company had subsided, and silence was restored, he leaned one arm on the elbow of his chair, and sticking the other akimbo, demanded, with a slight, but exceedingly sage motion of the head, and contraction of the brow, what was the moral of the story, and what it went to prove?

The story-teller, who was just putting a glass of wine to his lips, as a refreshment after his toils, paused for a moment, looked at his inquirer with an air of infinite deference, and, lowering the glass slowly to the table, observed that the story was intended most logically to prove--

"That there is no situation in life but has its advantages and pleasures--provided we will but take a joke as we find it:

"That, therefore, he that runs races with goblin troopers is likely to have rough riding of it.

"Ergo, for a country schoolmaster to be refused the hand of a Dutch heiress is a certain step to high preferment in the state."

The cautious old gentleman knit his brows tenfold closer after this explanation, being sorely puzzled by the ratiocination of the syllogism, while, methought, the one in pepper-and-salt eyed him with something of a triumphant leer. At length he observed that all this was very well, but still he thought the story a little on the extravagant--there were one or two points on which he had his doubts.

"Faith, sir," replied the story-teller, "as to that matter, I don't believe one-half of it myself." D. K.

THE MANY LEGENDS OF SLEEPY HOLLOW

THE NIGHT WAS A weapon. A blunt object best used against those of good faith and little sense. As with most things in life, fortune favored the rich and frowned upon the poor and down-trodden. Hence, it was that Jasper Badger found himself on an errand of utmost import with only the full moon and a lantern low on fuel to guide his way. Worse, there was little to be gained for the thirteen-year-old's travels through a forest choked with shadows and mystery.

Successfully completing his mission would not still the rumble in his stomach. (Oh, how the ripe scent of a late dinner wafting from the Stillwell's home threatened to derail his journey.) Theirs was the last house before the township ceded to immense forest. Deep, dark forest, full of restless spirits to hear the townsfolk tell it. The wall of trees about to swallow him whole turned the hunger in his stomach to worry, and he feared being sick. No, there was nothing about his mission that would fill his stomach or his pockets.

Any resolution to Jasper's folly would serve only one end. A debt repaid. It was an obligation that led the boy into the forest at an hour reserved for ne'er-do-wells and spirits aplenty. A single flake of snow and he might encounter shrieks from the Woman in White. Legend had it she was a local who perished in a blizzard and her spirit now cried a warning with every new snowstorm. The eerie, dark woods also welcomed the occasional ghostly funeral train.

The Hollow was renowned for its many restless spirits and kind folk. (Mostly kind, Jasper suffered frequent rough horseplay at the hands of larger classmates.) But one spirit's legend rose above all others. Even the most uneducated in town heard tales of Sleepy Hollow's most famous, and most oft seen spirit—a headless horseman. The soldier rode every night in search of a head lost to a cannonball in battle.

Many townsfolk who fought in battles themselves shared tales of war to those who might listen, especially after spending time in the local tavern. The liquids served inside the establishment loosened already loose tongues. Local boys were a captive audience and were happy to listen when their elders stumbled forth from the gathering spot. Those of uncertain feet shared stories and in turn revealed themselves to be haunted by spirits singularly different from those said to wander the Hollow.

Filled with fantasies about such battles (and when unaccompanied by parents who might scold them for reenacting such things), the boys would often side up and play war in the forest. There they hurled rocks in place of cannonballs. They did not throw them at one another (for even the dimmest understood the escalation possibilities), but through branches overhead where they landed close to the enemy troops.

Thrown properly, the loud pocks of rocks ricocheting off tree trunks and branches sounded much like the cannonballs that relieved the horseman of his head. The larger boys (uncharacteristically friendly while playing war, if only because they needed numbers to make it feel real) tossed rocks much larger than smaller boys could handle. The oversized rocks ripping through the trees were frightening. In those moments, the war became real. The boys could almost smell the gunpowder and corpses all around.

But a new legend had arisen in recent weeks. One relating to the man for whom Jasper owed his debt. There was one man who regularly stayed the hands of raucous brutes on the playground. For saving Jasper from many a thump against his skull, Jasper owed a debt to his favorite teacher.

Ichabod Crane.

The teacher had vanished on the very path that Jasper now walked, and at an almost identical hour. Jasper wanted nothing more than to run. Every strange sound in the dark forest was easy to mistake for a hoof's clop. But the boy refused to run, reserving his strength for when the fear became too much, and his legs were no longer his own. It would not take much more before his brain abandoned him and fear took over. Jasper barely maintained control of his shaking limbs as it was.

Ichabod had warned Jasper about the woods that day they spoke in the classroom. It was the last day he ever spoke to his favorite teacher. The man kept the boy after class while other students raced off after dismissal, eager to attend the quilting frolic that night.

"Jasper, I intend to secure the hand of Katrina Van Tassel tonight at the quilting frolic. Though I strongly believe in witches, spirits, and the headless horseman of these woods, there is one danger greater to me than all those."

"More dangerous than the headless horseman?" Jasper gulped.

"Indeed. The danger I speak of is singular to me. I believe the greatest consequence for my companionship with Ms. Van Tassel is a confrontation at the hands of Brom Bones, the brute who seeks Katrina's hand as well."

Jasper nodded. "He has chased her perhaps as long as the dead soldier has chased after his missing head."

"If something happens to me, I will require your services. Have I not stayed the hand of bigger students seeking merriment in your discomfort?" The boy nodded. "I did so because it is the right thing to do, However, given my precarious circumstances, I must insist that the favor be returned. I require your assistance under the light of the first full moon if I suffer sudden misfortune."

"How shall I know if misfortune visits itself upon you?"

"My absence. Have I ever missed a class?" Ichabod did not wait for an answer, it was clear the teacher never did nor never would miss a day with his students. "I have studied books some call blasphemous. In one such tome exists a remedy that may alter the course of my future. Can I count on you?"

Jasper nodded assent that day, but now, surrounded by dark forest, he shook his head, trying to forget the promise. The instructions provided at the time made little sense and frightened Jasper, but the boy committed them to memory and vowed to follow them to the word. Beneath his coat, Jasper held in place an item given to him by his teacher. The nature of the object unnerved him as much as the occasional owl hoot did.

The boy's free arm grew tired from holding a lantern aloft for so long. Moonlight lit the path well enough, but the lantern's flame would serve a secondary purpose later that night. *And soon*, Jasper hoped, for his heart grew as empty as his stomach. The further into the forest he travelled, the more snaps and crunches of footsteps other than his own seemed to echo from all sides. (And in the distance was that someone singing?)

Locals reported hearing someone unseen singing during their failed search for Ichabod Crane. All their efforts yielded nothing more than the discovery of Ichabod's borrowed saddle and a pumpkin. A music teacher, as well as an educator, some claimed the spirit of Ichabod chose the forest as a stage from where to perform.

To hear singing so late at night unnerved the boy. While Jasper appreciated the teacher enough to honor the man's last request, Jasper wished no part in spectral visits of any sort. But then, was that not the sole reason he carried the object under his coat? What was Ichabod up to? Something snapped again, much closer.

"Show yourself!" Jasper shouted.

The boy spun, hoping to identify anyone responsible for the snapped branches, but the moving lantern cast frightening shadows against the backdrop of night. Jasper was losing his legs. If his fear grew further, he would soon bolt on feet intent on outpacing his thundering heart. Gooseflesh covered every inch of his body despite his heavy winter coat.

Snap! To his right. Snick! To his left. Crunch! Dead behind. The forest came alive with sounds of spirits lost to the night. And underneath it all, the warbling voice of a man who in life looked much like a bird.

Then, in the distance, horse hooves galloped. Ichabod had warned Jasper about such a thing. Understanding the boy had no access to a steed, the teacher instructed Jasper to abandon the path in the face of horse hooves after sundown.

Jasper scrambled down the slope into the forest. The descent was dangerous, with tree roots and uneven ground hidden in darkness. The boy ran after reaching firm ground, but branches and tree trunks scraped him while navigating the dense forest. Jasper hoped the density of the forest would provide him cover from a horse too large to navigate the tight space. Even a horse that traveled between realms of both the living and the dead.

With one arm holding the lantern, he needed the other to navigate the woods more safely. That meant letting go of what he held under his coat. The boy tucked the item into his waistband while hoping it would not slip away into the night. Once settled he began to move again, pushing away low-hanging branches. A terrifying whinny sounded in the distance. The animal's cries sounded like crushed glass and rage. Riding parallel on the ridge above, the beast fell into a gallop that matched Jasper's stride.

Thick trees kept Jasper from confirming who rode the horse, but the clops were too thunderous for any normal steed. The clopping of the single beast on the ridge sounded as if the entire town's steeds had fallen into a stampede. Lost in fright, Jasper angled deeper into the forest but dared wander only so far, fearful of getting lost. Also, he needed to maintain his position to reach a very specific location, one that the headless horseman seemed intent on reaching as well.

As if the terror on the road above was not enough, something continued shaking branches in the distance, keeping time with the movements of the distant rider and himself. Whatever followed did so from somewhere deep in the forest. Who could it be? Or what? Jasper searched his surroundings while still running but glimpsed nothing more than shadows amidst puddles of moonlight.

Amidst branches snapping, and horse hooves clomping, another sound filled the night from somewhere behind him. Footsteps. But who would be out in the woods rather than on the main road? The individual somewhere behind him stumbled along on unsure feet like locals leaving the tavern. The thought of someone following him so closely frightened the boy, but that paled to what occurred next. Something whistled overhead. Branches crashed, snapped, and broke as an object soared through the air.

A cannonball?

Could it be? It was like the games the boys played with rocks, except this projectile came from a higher angle and at greater speed than even the biggest rocks the boys could muster. It had to be a real cannonball. Jasper was about to find out. The projectile headed his way. An object crashed down to his right. A near miss. Clods of forest floor exploded around Jasper who froze in terror.

The object exploded upon impact close enough that his lantern cast a glow over the orange object.

A pumpkin!

A pumpkin served as the cannonball. One launched with significant force from a rider who knew a thing or two about what cannonballs could do to the human head. When the pumpkin landed, its innards scattered like an old man's brains.

Singing sounded once again in the near distance. While scanning the area for the singer, Jasper glimpsed flashes of the branches shaking much like earlier. Jasper squinted but failed to identify the individual responsible. It was as if the boy had an invisible stalker.

More whistling alerted him to a second pumpkin projectile. Branches again cried out in protest as another orange cannonball arced high overhead. Jasper was under attack. Unlike playtime with the boys, the projectiles were arriving with deadly force. The second struck closer than the first, and Jasper found his legs again. He took off running while the horse on the ridge did the same. The pursuer at his rear picked up the pace as well. The race was on.

Three more pumpkins launched one after another. Branches and trunks, already half empty of leaves for the fall, snapped and bent in protest. The forest became a battlefield. A real one, unlike the playtime of his classmates. One pumpkin crashed so close that dirt and stringy pumpkin innards hit his face. He continued running while one whizzed over his shoulder. Another landed so close to his feet that he almost mis-stepped and fell. But he kept going.

More whistles from orange missiles filled the night. As he got a better look when they struck closer, jasper realized they were no mere pumpkins but Jack-o'-lanterns, lit by a flame that refused to extinguish in flight. Eerie carved faces grinned as if anticipating they would soon score a child-sized head.

Jasper's lantern clanked as he ran. The boy breathed heavy, growing tired from running and hoarse from screaming. Jasper looked up at the ridge and spotted his ultimate destination: the bridge. What would he do once there? What could he do?

More whistling. He noticed it too late. A glance over his shoulder revealed a projectile coming on fast. With no time to get out of the way he braced for the hit. But rather than the pumpkin striking him, something unseen struck him from behind, pushing him out of the way of the flying pumpkin.

Quickly recovering, Jasper eyed his rescuer and froze. Something utterly inconceivable stole rational thought from his mind. Jasper could not move, could not blink, could not understand what appeared before him. Tears filled his eyes. Pumpkins struck on all sides, and he simply allowed them to fall. Numb to the orange carnage. The forest had become a true war zone when at thirteen he witnessed something no boy was ever meant to see.

There were some soldiers in the taverns whose tongued would never loosen. Those men drank more than most and stumbled more wildly for it, but they refused to share with anyone what they experienced in battle. No amount of pleading from eager children ever elicited any stories from those men. Those soldiers simply finished their drinks and wandered off in a daze.

Jasper now understood those silent soldiers. The abomination appearing in front of Jasper gave him a better understanding of the soldiers. It also supplied him with a better understanding of why he had been unable to locate his pursuer. It also answered why the footsteps at his rear were so uncertain. Even now those footsteps plodded along, the pursuer bumping into tree after tree.

The bridge rose above the roadway above, bathed in a curtain of moonlight. Jasper had arrived at his destination but struggled to understand the mission's endgame. Especially in the face of that which saved him in the woods. (Face. Ha!) It was near the bridge where townspeople discovered Ichabod's belongings.

Jasper climbed the ridge on weary legs. There on the road the headless horseman loomed. The enormous figure sitting on a demonic steed held an enormous jack-o'-lantern. The sight of a man with no head normally would have sent Jasper running home to hide under covers. But he had just witnessed something more disturbing than the headless rider.

When Ichabod vanished, town leaders donated the man's books to the school except for Ichabod's witchcraft books. Church elders burned all of those. Except for the one hidden beneath Jasper's coat. While alive, Ichabod provided Jasper with the book and instructions for what needed to be done. Jasper had the required full moon, and there, under his coat, the dreadful book of spells. Jasper set the lantern down, retrieved the book, and opened it to a creased page where an incantation awaited a speaker.

The headless horseman's steed rose onto two legs, and the rider took aim with the pumpkin. There would be no missing this time. But the sight only elicited so much fear in the boy. For something equally terrifying awaited Jasper on his opposite side. For nearby, Ichabod Crane's head floated in the air, absent a body!

Ichabod's floating head was responsible for the fluttering branches off to his side during the journey. Because Jasper sought a whole body while scanning the forest earlier, he never spotted the head. The boy missed the forest for the trees. It was merely a head at his side the whole time, a floating one at that.

Out on the open road it was impossible to miss the head that nudged him clear of the flying pumpkin. From where Jasper stood he had a clear view of a head that bobbed on the air like a corked fishing line. The sight of Ichabod's floating head startled the horse and bought Jasper some time. The rider fought to settle a beast that should not have been frightened, as it was already dead. Maybe it did not know that.

While Jasper prepared to read the passage, his final pursuer came into view. Ichabod's lanky, headless body stumbled out of the forest. How it followed him through the woods without eyes to guide it, Jasper could not fathom. But then the man had sung as well. Perhaps Ichabod's eyes and ears still echoed in the veins of the separated body.

There was little time. If a thrown pumpkin did not take Jasper's head, the trio of spirits surrounding him threatened to still his heart from fear. Jasper felt ready to breathe his last. His mouth went dry, his knees knocked together and the heart in his chest beat at an unsustainable pace. Words on the page swam. He feared their power. The book and the page felt ancient.

Jasper cleared his raw throat and spoke the passage on the page. The words seemed to glow as he read each one. He fought to pronounce the mysterious words.

"Noctem plenam lunamque timore Praesens evolvit, medioque in corde recurrit. Vendo animam meam ut curet caput meum unde venit."

Before Jasper even finished the page, a glow overtook Ichabod's head. At the same time, the head appeared to catch a fresh current. Ichabod's body also assumed a glow before rising from the ground where it levitated several feet above the path. Jasper fought to hold onto reality in the face of madness, lest he lose his mind.

Did Ichabod wish to ensure he did not end up like the legendary horseman? Had the teacher suffered a premonition related to the night of the quilting frolic? Did Ichabod know all along his end would not come at the hands of a dueling suitor, but at the hands of the horseman? Surely it was the horseman who severed the good teacher into segments, was it not? Jasper wondered, unsure of what transpired the night Ichabod lost his head and life.

With his steed finally steadied, the headless horseman kicked the beast into action. The horse and rider raced straight toward Jasper! The boy cried out and cradled his own head trying to stall its departure. Jasper glimpsed the approaching spirit through elbows pressed tight against his skull. Ichabod's head continued floating on a luminescent trail. Ichabod's head and body tethered together from a distance, held in place by a bridge of light as solid as the bridge underfoot. A body and head reunion appeared in the works. But the headless horseman had other ideas.

The ground shook under the thundering hooves. Jasper had completed his good deed, even committed blasphemy in the name of his favorite teacher. But rather than enjoy a full stomach or riches, Jasper was about to become smaller than he already was by a head. The hooves were upon him now. Jasper awaited the snatch, but the hooves passed him by.

And a separate snatch occurred. The current of light tethered between his teacher's head and body became untethered when the headless horseman dropped the pumpkin and reached for Ichabod Crane's floating head.

The horseman took on a glow that extended all the way to Ichabod's surprised face. The teacher's head dangled by his hair in the horseman's grip. The light bridge now tethered Ichabod's head to the horseman's body. In a swift movement, the rider lifted the head and placed it where his own used to sit. In the chaos, Ichabod's body lost its glow, fell back to earth, and tumbled down the embankment into the forest.

Jasper had glanced toward the stumbling teacher's body. When he turned back, the horseman produced a hat from a saddlebag and place it atop his new head. Ichabod's face winked at Jasper and tilted the hat before the horse fell into a gallop and crossed the bridge, vanishing into the night.

Placing the witchcraft book in the center of the path, Jasper kicked the lantern over. The book went aflame. It ignited with great fury and what sounded like a chorus of a thousand voices, but soon the flame settled. The boy let it burn until the evil extinguished. Then he stamped it out and allowed the moonlight to guide him home.

Jasper never spoke of his adventure to anyone, even though the townsfolk would believe every word. After all, there were many legends about spirits in the woods. But one faded away over time as the encounters ceased. The headless horseman was never spotted again.

There was a new legend, however, one that joined the ranks of the Woman in White. It was the legend of a headless, spindly man stumbling about. Likely the body of their missing teacher. Jasper avoided those who spoke of such encounters. And as for himself, relieved of his obligation, Jasper avoided the woods entirely lest he himself become one of the many legends of Sleepy Hollow.

THE WOMAN IN WHITE

Time of death: six in the afternoon on December third in the year of our Lord 1785.

Time of life: eight in the evening on December third in the year of our Lord 1785.

~ so confirmed and signed by undertaker Milton Bland

I examined the card from years ago once again. It was my signature. I was there for the unimaginable event. As a former soldier, had I witnessed such a thing on the battlefield, it would have provided comfort and joy. To discover a fallen comrade suddenly breathing after a declaration of death would have boosted the morale of our entire militia. But battlefields were sorely lacking in hope or miracles and such a thing never occurred then, nor since.

It was five years ago in the comfort of my workspace that an unexplainable event transpired. There, in my undertaker chambers on a cold winter night—one of no particular distinct—a corpse in my charge decided she had other places to be.

The dead moan, blink, sigh, and release flatulence with stunning regularity. Occasionally, they sit up. Such machinations can occur after the soul has departed the body. This I know from experience. But to this day, only one woman ever took leave of my services.

Her name was Tabitha Pennywhistle, a comely woman who had drawn the affection of a local brute: Brom Bones. Pennywhistle, in her late twenties, an exquisite woman with dark hair and fine features, remained mysteriously single. Further, she rarely interacted with the citizens and neighbors, many of whom would have welcomed such interactions. Her untimely death brought only further mystery.

Such mysteries were my profession. (Well, one of them, I am a farmer by trade.) I serve as Sleepy Hollow's undertaker, a job that keeps me as busy as my occupational peers in the nearby city. I never believed (or had yet to) any of the superstitions that passed around the Hollow as freely as apples during fall harvest. Yet I could not argue how locals found their way to my basement workspace with uncommon frequency.

Understand that once deceased, I do not objectify any woman (or man) despite their inability to demand modesty in my presence. It would violate my duties for me to consider their physical state once their spiritual presence has left our world. My occupation demands I see them to the skin and examine their bared flesh for signs of foul play. While a smile from Ms. Pennywhistle whilst alive might have induced a dizziness to my counter and hope to my heart, as a corpse, she was simply part of my job.

Measure them to fit for the box, then seek a reasonable cause for why they ended up on my table. Before disrobing those in my care, I take steps to assuage my need to understand how they came to be deceased. Though not a man of medicine (and there is a great debate that undertakers should be) my time on the battlefield taught me that dead is dead.

I declared Ms. Pennywhistle dead immediately. Not only because she appeared quite so, but because of the state in which she arrived. Frozen solid.

Besides facilitating smooth transitions from this life to a person's last rest, my job is to record events as they occurred, and produce a concise record for historical fact. Five years have passed since Ms. Pennywhistle first haunted my thoughts in a manner befitting the Hollow. Unable to fully understand then the events as they unfolded, I now seek with time's clarity to put to rest the memory of the woman, if not her body. It is heretofore my intention to submit a last record of note regarding the missing woman once left in my care.

I intend to embark on a quest to secure answers to a long unsolved mystery. As this venture promises to place me in great peril, I hereby commit to paper in advance all that transpired until now, lest something happen to me while seeking a woman who remains missing. (And if persistent rumors prove true, my sanity is at stake. For if one comes to believe that spirits roam the earth, does it not mean one's own senses have left the earth as well?)

As word of the incident got out, church officials absconded with my original records. All that remained behind was a customary card to be placed alongside the body which recorded time of death. Not only did the church whisk away the records, but a roguish individual purporting to be from the church approached me in an aggressive and ungodly manner. He strongly suggested I remain silent in all things Pennywhistle.

I honored their clumsy requests until now. But after five years of curiosity eating at my heart, I can no longer abide by their wishes. What follows is the record of the night I processed the body and my subsequent search for the truth.

Attestation of Milton Bland regarding the disappearance of formerly deceased Tabitha Pennywhistle.

Despite being of recent questionable mind and body, I declare the following events as they occurred to be truthful and accurate to the best of my recollections. What follows is the recounting of my undertaker notes from the night when Ms. Pennywhistle abdicated her deathbed responsibilities. (Responsibilities of any corpse include remaining deceased up to and through burial.)

Processing the frozen corpse was a dreadful thing, even for one accustomed to such affairs. The human spirit must be the lightest part of any being. Its departure leaves behind a shell of surprising weight. Corpses, under any circumstances, are stubbornly heavy. But frozen water added additional weight to one who was rather petite in life. Brom assisted me in lifting her onto my exam table.

The woman perished in a kneeling position, arms at her sides. That meant her knees were not only frozen in a bent position, but secured there by mortis as well. That left two options: place her on her side or station her on her back but low down on the table where her legs could dangle over its edge. Examination was easier on her back, so I chose the latter. With the corpse positioned, I asked Brom for the circumstances behind the discovery.

A man of many hats, Brom favored a fur fox-tail hat during the winter months. He removed the cap and held it to his chest before recounting the tale of discovering the woman who he oft wooed but never wed.

"There is no better horseman in the land than I. Agreed?"

"Aye," I said.

Brom smiled, a man unafraid to accept a compliment despite standing before the deceased object of his affection. Nary a one-track mind had I ever seen. Brom continued.

"As the best horseman to roam the lands, I consider it my duty to travel to the furthest outskirts of the Hollow to warn citizens that the furious hand of winter has descended upon the town."

I did not bother to remind Brom that we were already under several feet of snow from previous storms, and that more was normal during the winter months. I found his declaration suspect. Courtesy dictated Ms. Pennywhistle invite Brom in for a spot of tea in such weather if the man knocked during a storm. I remained silent about my suspicions so Brom could continue.

"My muscles, the envy of many, are oft times beyond my control. So, it was when I first knocked on the door of Ms. Pennywhistle, I deemed it unlikely she had failed to hear me. And deemed it even more unlikely she would ignore me. Fearing foul play, I promptly entered her home, for who would not wish me to do so in such circumstances? Her home proved immaculate. I expected no less. But the woman's absence prompted a search which led me to her sleeping quarters. I assure you had I discovered her sleeping, I would have receded to the living quarters until she woke. I visited her home with no ill intentions. Alas, she was nowhere to be found which filled me with concern."

So says the man who faced the possibility of being snowbound for a day or more if the storm worsened, I thought. I considered the man's reasoning quite suspect, but any ill intent he might have planned, vanished when the object of his affection turned up deceased. I refocused the conversation, asking directly for the physical condition in which Brom found her.

"While exiting her home, I spotted an empty hook. A small thing that may have gone unnoticed by a lesser man, but to one as savvy as myself, I realized what likely belonged there. A bucket which would serve one purpose, retrieving water from her well. I thought it was worth looking for her well. But by the time I stepped outside, the storm had grown exponentially worse. If you are unfamiliar with Ms. Pennywhistle's land, it is vast. The field behind her house is larger than most local plots of land. But then I guess as a farmer you are aware, and perhaps such a lot haunts you with envy. Knowing roughly where the above ground well was located, I made my way through deep snow until I kicked the bucket. It was my foot that struck the thing. I dug through the snow and found the empty pail."

Brom had said plenty and I understood where this was heading. Most citizens prepared for storms with a lethargic disinterest as blizzards were routine. Sadly, it appeared Ms. Pennywhistle failed to secure enough water from her well before the storm hit.

Brom looked to the woman as if the memory haunted him. "The storm had already swept up her footprints. One might think it impossible to locate a missing person in such a blizzard, but as you know, I am savvier than most. My observation skills exceed those of lesser townsfolk. Squinting through the flurry, I spied a snowman in the near distance, one minus coal for eyes, and no carrot to be found. The figure stood waist high to me."

Brom gestured to his waist. Then he swung an arm as if wiping away snow.

"I gave the fanciful thing a dusting and soon uncovered a most unfortunate sight. Ms. Pennywhistle served as the bones of the snow sculpture. She was in an upright kneeling position, arms at her sides. The good woman not only wore a fresh coat of snow, but had frozen to the ground, trapped in place by water spilled from the bucket. It took some effort, even for a man of my strength, to free her. I fashioned a sled from items at her house, attached her to the rear of my horse and delivered her here. A most unfortunate night, I must say. Now I leave her in your care," Brom said.

The man was as thorough a storyteller as he was a braggart. No medical degree was needed to understand the poor woman succumbed to the elements. I would have preferred some company while working but I needed to disrobe the individual. Those in my care deserved privacy equivalent to that they would expect while breathing. Brom leaving was for the best. Besides, what was my job if not to always work frightfully alone? I bid Brom Bones a somber goodbye and allowed him to see himself out.

Ms. Pennywhistle's contorted position made simple undressing impossible. The situation forced me to cut away her evening gown (one not designed for the weather which likely contributed to her demise). Though difficult, I snipped away the frozen cloth.

With her skin fully exposed, it was time to examine the body. There was little need to determine cause of death, but the exams provided a secondary function. A proper examination helped determine if any cosmetic assistance was needed to ensure the corpse looked its best for any public viewings. After processing the body, I would promptly dress her once again in fresh clothes as hers were cut away.

But dressing her in such a twisted position would prove more difficult than the undressing. There was only one thing I could do. I reached into a nook hidden in my basement wall and retrieved a hidden bottle of whiskey. The bottle was one "tool" of my job, only to be used in the direst situations. This was one.

Rather than wait until the poor woman thawed, I considered it best to get on with it, but that meant changing her position. Because the church made unavailable the original notes from that night, I plan to retell the events to the best of my memory. The following is the full recounting of the dreadful circumstances from that fateful night.

I caution that the following may prove uncomfortable for those unfamiliar with the machinations of corpse handling. The actions taken that night out of necessity disturbed me then as well as now. But the details are an important part of the record to understand my upcoming course of action. Given the sensitive nature of the following account, I shall describe the morbid affair on a separate page. This will allow those with a low constitution the ability to merely imagine how her time on my table went.

Attestation to the circumstances behind the postmortem examination of Tabitha Pennywhistle

With some struggle, I turned the corpse over onto its stomach. That position resulted in the legs facing the ceiling. The body remained low on the table however, with her kneecaps positioned over the table's edge. Before completing the task at hand, I needed to fix the legs.

There was no good alternative other than grabbing heels and pulling. That was what I did, but her legs remained stubbornly fixed. Being gentle was no longer an option. I grabbed the heels once again and put my body weight behind it and pulled while falling back.

The corpse legs trembled under my body weight and effort. With twin snaps, the legs released their tension. The sudden release caused me to stumble. I instinctively held the corpse legs to stop my fall. In grim fashion, the limbs followed my trajectory and snapped a second time, this time at the kneecaps which bent in a direction they were not designed to. I fell to the ground on my rump.

Before I could reorient myself, I leaped to my feet, prodded by the sound of draining liquid. I feared my bottle of spirits had tipped in the chaos, but the only spilled spirits were those dripping from her body. Or from the back of her knees to be precise. Not only had the kneecaps broken along the edge of the table, but the skin on the back of her knees ruptured. The corpse bled freely from the backs of the knees.

A frozen body did not mean frozen blood. Red gushed from the grisly torn knees. (But the finest dirt floor available absorbed the warm liquid just fine and would be easy enough to shovel away later.) I allowed the corpse to drain over the sand.

The torn and dislocated knees were a grisly sight. The corpse's legs dangled like rubber over the edge of the table. Once the blood stopped its aggressive pour, I turned the woman over onto her back and lifted her whole body onto the table which straightened her legs. Something must have loosened in the anatomy through the breaks and ruptures, for her feet fell into a most unnatural position. The left foot faced left and the right to the right, heels touching. A ballerina position if I remembered correctly from a holiday dance event I attended long ago in the city. (Though I remembered little of the underwhelming production.) Feet were not meant to turn that way living or dead in my professional opinion.

A melancholy overtook me as I considered her cause of death. The image of Pennywhistle being found in the form of a snowman (snow woman?) haunted me. Was Ms. Pennywhistle frozen to the ground while alive, unable to move, trapped in spilled water? If so, how long had she remained alive as the snow covered her? Or had she immediately succumbed to the cold before becoming a woman in white?

No undertaker, even one with a medical degree, could ever know with certainty. Those questions would remain unanswered. Per my job responsibilities, I examined whether there were any other injuries visible (beyond the horrific broken and bleeding legs that occurred postmortem) There appeared nothing foul about her body. With the examination finished, it was time to dress her. But I first needed to dispose of the blood to ensure it did not get on her new clothes. I would start by shoveling away the affected dirt on the floor. I also needed to decide which garment to bury her in.

Understand that many consider it poor form (and dreadfully bad luck) to bury loved ones in the clothes they perished in. Most families brought fresh clothing considered more proper for burial. If a victim's clothing was serviceable (unlike the frozen and cut garments of Ms. Pennywhistle), I saved them to repurpose for others with lesser means for burial. With no known family, I would need to dress her with something on hand. I had a rack at the ready nearby on which hung various men's and women's clothing.

But I needed that shovel first, so I pardoned myself to the women, ascended the stairs, threw on a coat and headed out in the monstrous storm. The barn loomed large in the distance, but my house quickly vanished from sight at my rear. Seeing how fast it faded to white clued me in on how easily Ms. Pennyworth could have succumbed to such a storm.

Foolishly I left the house without gloves, and the bitter cold numbed my hands. Once I reached the barn and found my shovel, I was eager to return to the warmth of the fire burning in my house. But soon after leaving the barn, panic overtook me. I could not find my house!

So thoroughly white was the blanket of snow that it wrapped itself around my head, or at least my vision. My own footsteps behind me vanished under new snow as fast as I made them. Both avenues of shelter vanished from sight. If I chose a wrong direction in which to walk I would miss the structures and succumb to the elements like the woman in my care.

Then the strangest thing occurred. Something struck me with tremendous force. So hard it was as if Brom Bones himself thrashed me. The strike spun me around and I almost fell down into the snow. In the same moment as the inexplicable strike, a frigid wind swept over me, one that chilled me to the very bones of my toes. Never had I experienced such cold; it was as the hand of death had reached out and caressed my heart.

Understanding inaction meant demise, I chose to walk in the direction I faced after the unexplained collision. I stumbled forward and, with great luck, discovered my home. Once inside, I left my coat on to recover from the bitter cold while stomping down the steps so loudly, that like Brom mentioned, I feared I might wake the dead. After returning to my workspace, I had to consider whether I had done such a thing. For nothing was as I left it.

Ms. Pennywhistle was gone!

All that remained on the table was a puddle of water where she had partially thawed. But as for the woman, one of both beauty and misfortune, she was absent from my table!

I mentioned before how the dead do many things, including sitting up. I feared the woman had done so but had nothing to hold her in position because of the broken knees, Perhaps the body could not support itself and she fell off to one side. But an inspection of the entire basement proved fruitless. The body was missing. Along with a wedding dress.

If any other garment had gone missing, I might not have noticed. The missing item belonged to a bride who perished in a carriage strike on her wedding day. Because the groom proposed to a new bride before the burial of the first, the family wanted no connection to the cad. The family brought other clothes for the unfortunate lady and the dress was left behind. White, with puffy shoulders, the dress was not overly fancy, a modest garment for a family of modest means. Given the circumstances, the wedding dress had remained in my chambers, hanging amongst the other abandoned pieces of clothing. Until now. Like the corpse of one Ms. Tabitha Pennywhistle, the bridal dress was gone.

Immediately I sought a rational explanation. Tales were plentiful of people falling through ice and being revived long after they should have been unrevivable. Perhaps the ice froze the human spirit long enough to give some a second chance. Did Ms. Pennywhistle thaw and wake, only to find herself in a dreadful immodest state? Unclothed and in unfamiliar surroundings would prove a nightmare scenario for even those with hardy constitutions. She would have dressed immediately.

But her legs! Oh, how they had snapped. Blood had flowed freely, with enough lost that it would have dizzied the strongest individual into unconsciousness. Besides, it was one thing for her to wake, another to walk. It would have been impossible in her condition.

The shovel in my hand reminded me of my mission, and that memory provided a clue. Blood. She had not ceased bleeding by the time I sought the tool, but it had slowed to a trickle. I searched the floor and there, beyond the drying puddle at the base of the table, I glimpsed the impossible.

Damp footprints and a blood trail led to where the dress previously hung. I dropped the shovel, raised my lantern, and followed the trail which led up the stairs. Despite my disbelief in superstition, my hands shook as I climbed the stairs. The footprints led to my front door. That she found her way directly to the exit without knowing the layout of my sizeable home shocked me.

Was she alive upon entry and mapping the path to the basement? Any scenario still did not resolve how she came to walk with damaged legs.

Though all ballerinas practiced the first position, that of turned-out feet, no dancers walked about in such a pose. It was merely a starting point for the dance number ahead. Yet based on her footprints, Ms. Pennywhistle walked heel to heel. What gait would that produce while she stumbled about? The thought brought fresh shivers up my spine.

The path led straight to my front door which confirmed she exited. But when? Had we crossed paths when I retrieved the shovel? It would have been easy for me to miss her during the storm. I opened the door to gale force winds. The storm had worsened. If she had fallen under the effects of the storm in its infancy, (and survived by some miracle), then how would she fare in a storm such as this?

"Ms. Pennywhistel!" I yelled, but the storm swallowed my voice.

A warm fire at my back beckoned me to abandon my search especially with nothing but blinding white coldness beyond the threshold. It was no storm to set foot in, but curiosity burned within my heart. I had to know how it was the woman came to exit my workspace. Lifting my lantern, I stepped outside.

"Ms. Pennywhistle!" I cried while silently cursing Brom for leaving so quickly.

The wind swept so fiercely that I fought to stay on my feet. It came in a burst and brought enough snow onto my lantern that I had to wipe the glass clear because the world had gone dark. Once clear, the lantern's glow showed only white against a blanket of night, as if I existed in a void, a moment in between heartbeats. The surroundings induced in me a great panic. There was no house, no barn, no woman with twisted legs. Only white, and it threatened to embrace me to my last.

"Screeeeeeee!"

A horrendous cry sounded in my ear, as if the devil himself stood at my side. I turned, desperate, confused. Afraid. Was the wind so powerful that it could make such a vile sound?

"Screeeeeeee!"

Again, so close to my ear it was as if someone shared a whisper, but in the form of a scream. The cry rattled eardrums and bones. It had to be the Devil, for the voice carried within it a great sorrow. Despite how afraid I was, the cry threatened to move me to tears. Never so sorrowful a wail had I ever heard.

"Screeeeeeee!"

The cry had not changed from the others, yet somehow it was different. Within the voice it carried an implied threat. Great fear struck my heart. I failed to understand how I came about such knowledge, but I understood that if I did not run, the thing would end me.

I do not believe in superstition, but for the first time since living in the Hollow, I feared losing my head. My lantern danced as I ran, the metal handle clinking in time with my knees rattling in fear. The path led me straight to my door. I rushed inside, set the lantern down and slammed the door.

Wham!

I cried out in fright. Something outside struck the door with incredible force. I pushed back but the door insisted on opening. A second blow struck so hard it hurled me away, sending me to the floor on my haunches. Wind and snow swept into my home as the door burst open. I rose to close it and glimpsed a frightful sight.

In the distance a woman in a wedding gown stared me down with eyes of burning coal. Wind swept a burst of snow into my face. By the time I had wiped it away, the image was gone as if never there at all.

Investigation into the Woman and White legend as it relates to missing person Ms. Tabitha Pennywhistle

For those who wisely avoided the previous passage which documented the brutal fate of Ms. Pennywhistle, allow me to recap briefly. A deceased woman left her designated spot in my undertaker's workshop. That is roughly what occurred and reading the previous passage provides no answers as to how it happened. I will admit, however, those events tested my previously firm beliefs that tales of spirits wandering the Hollow were nothing more than mere superstition.

In the five years since that night, I faced many inquiries. Both the church and town officials investigated my actions with no courtesies given to my years of professionalism prior to that one event. Their heavy-handedness resulted in my eventual resignation as an undertaker.

Rather than hire someone new, Sleepy Hollow elders contracted out undertaker services to the nearby city. For such a sleepy Hollow, we had more than our share of misfortune (mostly tied to the local legends). It was determined that a larger city was better able to perform more thorough examinations (up to and including proof of death).

But in the winters since my scandalous loss of a corpse, a new legend was born. I tried not to attribute the emerging legend to my folly as an undertaker, but how could one not question if their actions played a part in something so unnerving?

Since that night with stunning regularity, at the first sign of any storm, a voice wailed loud and mournful. The cries carried on the wind through the entire Hollow. It was enough to drive most citizens into their homes to ride out storms in safety. Failure to shelter in place could result in an encounter with a ghostly apparition in white.

Twice on the night of the Pennywhistle disappearance, forces unknown to me steered me in the direction of my home during a blizzard. Acts of God, or acts of a missing corpse? Some brave, or lost townsfolk who found themselves out in the elements occasionally caught chilling glimpses of a woman in white roaming nearby fields. Several citizens mentioned how the woman had pointed. In such instances, those fleeing the horrific sight felt compelled to escape in the direction she indicated. Each time, it landed them back on the path from which they had inadvertently strayed.

Ms. Pennywhistle in life was a stunning woman, enough to draw Brom's attention. Yet those who glimpsed the Woman in White spoke of sheer terror during the brief encounters. Mostly because of the strange jerky nature of her stride, and the deep dark black and red pools of her eye that burned like coal. I had glimpsed the same for mere moments and could not reconcile that image with the stunning beauty of Ms. Pennywhistle.

To remove any doubt that they were the same, I needed to locate the Woman in White. Over the past five years, I studied signs of impending blizzards. As I aged, my back assisted me in predicting storms. The winds that arrived in advance of the snow sent twinges of discomfort down my spine, a result from so many years lifting bodies.

Several storms had already blanketed the Hollow with snow, but storms like ghostly legends appeared to favor the night. I preferred to do my research in the light of day, and finally one such storm was on its way at midday.

Flakes started to fall by noon, too late to cancel classes at the local schoolhouse. That was fortuitous as there was one individual whom I needed to talk to prior to my planned adventure. A man relatively new to town. One wise in both scholarly studies, and studies of a more arcane nature.

Ichabod Crane.

After bundling up, I made my way to the school as it let out for the day. Children raced past, some greeting me with such merriment that I momentarily forgot about all the unpleasantries the day ahead promised. Snowballs flew about with a little too much zeal, forcing me to scold some of the older children who should have known better. They respectfully ceased their roughhousing and went on their way. I entered the school where Ichabod shared a strange book with a young boy from town.

Jasper Badger. A bright boy, knowledgeable in many things. Word travelled in the Hollow about those with impressive skills, intellectual or otherwise. The boy was from a poor family so suffered malnourishment. The teacher standing alongside the boy looked like two sticks having a conversation.

As for the book the two studied, it was a foul looking thing, with a dark black spine resembling rot. Hieroglyphics of an unreadable nature lined the same spine. The book was open atop Ichabod's desk when I entered, but the teacher closed the book upon spotting me and urged the boy to leave. Jasper looked out the window with concern before choosing the exit. I sensed his concern and assured him that the snowball throwing students had already moved on. The boy lit up, thanked me, and ran out into the snow.

"Milton Bland. To what do I owe the pleasure?" Ichabod patted down his own body. "I am not dead, am I?"

"Now, Ichabod, you know I am no longer the undertaker. Have not been since before your arrival in town."

"Not to hear the townsfolk tell it. If I were to drop right here, who do you think they would seek to clean up the mess?"

"I suppose. Are you expecting a perishable moment in your near future?"

"If Brom Bones has his way, aye," Ichabod said.

I grinned, remembering Brom's fascination with Pennywhistle and how quickly it faded. The new woman in Brom's sights was Katrina Von Tassell. Ichabod Crane pursued the same woman. Nodding in recognition of the conflict, I tried to put the teacher at ease.

"Brom is a fickle man when it comes to affairs of the heart. The secret is outlasting his infatuation until his eye catches someone new," I said.

"Were it that simple. Speaking of such things, thank you for putting Jasper's mind at ease just now. The larger boys in class often use their size as a weapon of cruelty against the frail lad. I fear Brom intends the same for me out of frustration that the beautiful Ms. Von Tassel dares to look my way. But none of that is why you are here."

"Indeed. I seek your counsel in a particular subject. You are wise to make light of your interest in witchcraft. If you showed too much enthusiasm the church would engage with you and the school in a most unkind manner. I wish you to be forthright with me on your knowledge of such things."

"The Lady in White. You seek her."

"How did you know?"

"A storm bears down on our town. Most spirits said to roam these lands vanish in such conditions. Few are the travelers in weather such as this. Only the Lady in White appears with or without an audience, mindless of who might be foolish enough to brave the elements," Ichabod said.

"Aye. You are wise."

Ichabod turned the book on his desk toward me. Hieroglyphics, in a scrawl most unfamiliar rose from the cover much like the spine. The binding appeared made of burnt flesh and the lettering rose like clotted blood across its face.

Regardless of the book's contents, its appearance was off-putting. I wondered why a teacher would share such a thing with a student, but that was not my concern. I needed answers. Failure to act quickly would mean darkness. Ichabod continued.

"What some misunderstand about witchcraft is that a list of spells is not to be combined and used by one individual. Books of spells are for as many people as there are pages. Given my worries with Brom, I discovered one such page that might assist me in a worst-case scenario. Jasper may be the one to assist me in the future if needed. Not many can read Latin. Do you?"

"Yes," I said.

Ichabod flipped through the book. Every page was red ink on black and the volume unnerved me a great deal. I did not believe in such things, yet what harm would there be in using superstition to chase a superstition? He stopped at a certain page and gestured to it.

"What language do you see?" Ichabod asked.

"Latin."

Ichabod nodded. "Jasper saw the same on a page I shared with him. He is a strong student, advanced past the others. He is currently learning the language in between his other studies."

"Latin is common in older volumes. Why does the language matter?"

"Because there is no Latin in this entire volume. No English either, for that matter."

It was clearly in Latin. I scoffed at the man. "That is absurd."

"See for yourself. Turn the pages."

I consider myself an educated man, but Ichabod proved correct. Every other page in the book was indecipherable to me. I returned to the page in question and saw both the hieroglyphics, but somehow Latin as well. It was a curious thing.

"The language on the cover and inside predates Akkadian, a language born before even Latin. If one can read a page in this book, then it was designed for them. Or someone with a similar need."

Ichabod tore the page free from the volume. Black dust flowed in a tiny cyclone toward the ceiling as if the ink had left the pages one letter at a time. Ichabod handed the single sheet to me. My heart leaped from my chest as the classroom door burst open with a startling thump. Wind and snow swept into the classroom, followed by the sound of my destiny.

"Screeeeeee!"

Even Ichabod, a man brave enough (if not foolish) to stand up against Brom Bones, shivered at the cry emanating from somewhere in the storm. Ichabod stored the book away, grabbed his satchel, and put on his coat. It fit the bony man as if he were a coatrack. I stood there listening to the first few shrieks of the Woman in White, while Ichabod wrestled with the door.

"A little help, my good man?"

I shook myself out of a fugue, pocketed the page and rushed to the door. We stepped through and I helped him close it. A chain and padlock were ready on the other side. We locked the door as if it contained pirate treasure.

Ichabod stepped back and nodded at our handiwork. "Easier with two, I must say. The door only blows open in the worst of storms. That we struggled to secure it suggests you are in for wicked weather for your quest. As for the school, the chains might rattle ceaselessly but the door will hold. Now back to your mission. You wish not to believe in a world beyond our understanding."

I nodded. "In a world of natural order and science, everything has an answer to its own riddle."

'Why then, faced with certain peril, do I pursue the beautiful Katrina Von Tassell? Love? One cannot see love, or touch it, but it makes me sing, it makes me dance when I would rather not. It makes me want to walk hand in hand and look at the moon and stars while she and I plan a future. Do you believe in love, Mr. Bland?"

I considered myself a lonely man. Work had always consumed my life alongside my studies, but there was a woman I longed for from a time in my past. I had experienced it, so in love, I believed. Though love is as elusive as it is intangible. I nodded.

"Then you already believe in that which cannot be seen. The page I gave you will lower a veil. Many refuse to believe in the Headless Horseman who races through town in search of his missing head. But most refuse to believe out of fear of the unknown. Easy to deny something exists if one never strays far from their front door. But the Woman in White? None can deny the cries that flood the land."

"Aye," I said and cinched my coat. Despite my strong desire to disbelieve that the Woman in White existed, I could not argue that the cry unnerved me to my core.

"Your disbelief in such things could forever leave you with unanswered questions. But that page in your pocket will force you to see beyond the veil. Just understand, there is no turning back once you read it. Now we shall both take leave lest the storm pick us off one by one."

"Thank you," I said, leaping when the woman screamed again. The sound was everywhere all at once. When I turned back, Ichabod was gone, vanished in the snow so quickly he could have been an apparition flickering from sight.

The skies were dark gray, but enough daylight remained to guide me as I set out on foot. Cyclones of white accompanied me on my walk, and the winds threatened to lift me up, perhaps fly me to my destination. Soon enough I arrived at the former home of Ms. Pennywhistle.

Time had not been kind to the place. It remained unoccupied since her passing. The front door tilted to one side, dangling on a single hinge. Snowbanks filled the partially open space. Broken glass shards lined the window casings like wild animal teeth.

The property remained in her name if only because my death certificate was pulled by local officials. Without a body, the woman remained owner. Not that anyone would have moved in. Those in the Hollow were far too superstitious to settle into such an unsettling place. Despite the impressive lot of land the house sat on, it faded into the town's memory, forgotten, only to be reconsidered at the beginning of every storm.

"Screeeeeee!"

I spun. The cry was in my ear. I often wondered if the cry grew louder in proximity. It had, which meant I was close. I peered across the white landscape and caught a glimpse. A momentary view, but it could have been the flutter of a gown. Or simply more snow.

Either way, the movement appeared near my planned destination. It was not only her property I planned to visit, but the place where Brom found the woman. As I neared the well, a woman ran past! Or so it seemed.

A figure in white ran through the snow, lifting her dress to allow a better run. But oh, how she ran. The sight brought a chill to my heart. I had long wondered how the woman might walk on such feet and I saw it in action, if even for a moment. The figure that raced past appeared human, but inhuman. It vanished in white.

"Where are you?" I cried out.

Though a rational man, I tried to put my preconceived beliefs aside as Ichabod had urged. The well rose off to my right. Like many wells in the area, a circle of stone served as a base that rose several feet above the ground to keep people and animals from falling inside. Above even the stones rose a pyramid of logs that angled from the sides of the well only to meet at the top where they were tied off. The pyramid style covering allowed for easy access and had hooks on which to secure buckets. The Hollow would never get enough snow to bury the structure, but to fully coat it was another thing. The well itself was caked in white but maintained its proper form.

I moved toward it with uneasy thoughts. What had I just seen in the snow? Had I seen the Woman in White? Was she real? Hard to say from such a quick glimpse. I had to know. Reluctantly, I reached into my pocket and retrieved the page given to me by the honorable gentleman Crane.

"Screeeeeee!"

Again, the voice was there, but dancing on a wind that whipped all about. This close I sensed doom in the cadence. The page shook in my hand, if not from the relentless winds, then from fear. I read the words in Latin, almost in a whisper at first. It felt blasphemous to even hold such a document.

"Screeeeeee!"

The cry drowned out my voice, so I raised it, yelling into the storm, committed to the words on the page. The Latin flew freely off my tongue. As I finished the chant, the wind whipped more violently, almost knocking me off my feet. The snow blew singularly in my direction, blinding me. I battled to stand upright. It was as if the words disturbed the very hollow itself. I could not see a thing.

Understanding there would be no help, I cried out anyway. A mistake. My mouth filled with ice and snow, quickly, forcefully, as if the boys throwing snowballs earlier aimed at my face. The wind ripped the page from my hands and it swirled off into the white.

Never had a storm in the Hollow struck so fast and with such intensity. I felt no longer of the earth and feared I would soon face my occupational brethren on a table somewhere in a distant month's time when the world thawed, if it ever would. The cold rattled my bones.

I fell to my knees and fought to clear my throat. There was so much packed snow it no longer melted under my body heat, forcing me to reach my hand into my mouth to remove segments of the obstruction. I pulled a snowball's worth and spit out the rest. Once able to breath again, I noticed I knelt in the manner Ms. Pennywhistle had in her last hours.

Everything fell silent. The wind ceased wailing, and the snow settled into a graceful and mute fall. My eyes cleared, able to see once again. I staggered to my feet, only to stagger once again. A snowman appeared directly in front of me, one shaped like a kneeling woman, arms at her side. The shape was so defined, an artist could have carved it from marble.

But that was not all. To my right rose an exact replica. Another to my left, to my front, and at my rear. The snow figures dotted the landscape, filling almost every foot of the massive field. They stretched as far as I could see. The world's volume had muted. No more wind, not even the sound of my heavy breathing or my thundering heart made its way to my ears. A worry set in that I had succumbed to the elements. How else to explain the sight before me?

Or more accurately, sights. It was impossible. In all things between Heaven and Earth, never had such wonderment left me so dumbfounded. The impossible had become possible in a moment of calm in a storm. I knew Ms. Pennywhistle's form. Though I had not studied her body (in accordance with my professional ethics) I was intimately familiar enough to recognize it.

Now, there in the field she used to call home, Ms. Pennywhistle's corpse lay covered in white, on her knees, dozens of times over. I questioned my sanity, blinked my eyes, but the strange vision remained. I needed to know, to understand. That meant to touch, to feel, to determine what was of this world and what belonged elsewhere.

I reached my hand out, brushed at the snow on what would have been the face of the snow person. The head fell away, a chunk of snow landing in a puff of its own making. The headless figure reminded me of the tales of a Headless Horseman that no longer felt farfetched. But in the end, the mysterious figure was nothing more than packed snow.

Moving on to the next, I once again brushed its face. It too fell away, headless in a field, but nothing more than snow, the figure an echo of the woman that it mimicked. My legs shook as I moved onto the next. I knew not what I looked for, only that I needed to understand. But I could not.

Though the storm had vanished as mysteriously as the figures had appeared, the cold remained. I had limited time to find my answers, so I moved more quickly. Advancing from one kneeling woman made of white to the next, I swiped at the heads. Decapitating dozens in mere minutes. Some heads remained on shoulders, with only the faces falling away, giving the disturbed figures blank stares.

There were so many silent sentries of snow in the field, it was impossible to explore them all. And even if it were possible, to what end would I inspect each? They were all the same as the ones I had already examined. Or were they? Remembering my clumsy actions in my undertaker's chamber that resulted in a flow of blood, I searched the figures anew.

I trudged through the snow with renewed vigor, looking for something specific. It was only when I explored a distant portion of the field and returned toward the well that I saw it. It should have been the first place I checked. Possibly in the very spot where Ms. pennywhistle perished, one snow figure differed from the others. This one bled at the knees where the figure kneeled.

Circling around to its front, I reached out and wiped at the snow. The head did not crumble, rather chunks of snow fell away to reveal two closed eyes, circled by skin of blue, a woman frozen both in the field and in time. Was it possible she awaited a second rescue? Was the Woman in White ready to be buried for good?

Then the eyes opened! In them I saw a darkness deeper than any I ever encountered. Even corpses had more life in their own dull eyes. These stared at me, through me, and possibly into worlds beyond my understanding. I screamed but could not move. Before I had finished my frightful cry, the woman joined in with her own.

"Screeeeeee!"

The sound cut through the Hollow. Cries of the terrified and a terrifier. Worse, the woman's mouth remained covered in snow, yet she cried louder than I. Her voice found the wind which had suddenly reappeared. The storm struck with renewed fury. Ambient sound returned to the Hollow. The wind amplified her voice and buried mine.

I ran at that moment, like a man possessed. There was no good to come from confronting the woman, nor investigating her health. There was no Pennywhistle any longer. Now there was only the Woman in White.

"Go away!" I yelled, a foolish thing to say.

The woman would do as she pleased. Unlike those of us with beating hearts, the Woman in White traipsed between worlds, able to do as she pleased, up to and including forming hundreds of icy edifices on her property. HER property. I did not belong. Nor did any man. It was well past the time for me to take my leave.

Running through snow proved taxing, but I neared her house. It came up suddenly, invisible in the storm until I grew closer. I looked back to check for a pursuer. The sculptures were gone, or at least lost in the white.

I slowed, feeling I had left the horrific sight behind. Then I looked down and noticed spots of blood near my feet. So close to where I stood.

"Skreeeeeee!"

That was my cue. I ran again. Somewhere off to one side, I glimpsed a woman wearing a wedding dress dancing through the storm on broken legs. I ran faster, off the property, through the

Hollow, past the closed Tavern, past the school, and to my home. I fought to breathe through the effort, but my legs would not stop.

Once inside my home, I found one of the bottles from my time as an undertaker. and emptied it of its contents, (I no longer stored the drink in my former workspace but in my pantry.) There was little liquid left and it failed to give me courage. I disposed of the bottle and descended to my basement.

The tools of my former trade still filled the room. I had allowed the space to fall into neglect but had never cleared the space of objects related to my former profession. It was time to bury the remnants of that life. Or burn them. I scooped up all the clothes that remained hanging on my rack. They had long since served their purpose. The bundle weighed me down making it difficult to ascend the stairs, especially after a run. But I needed to occupy my mind with tasks to move on from the horror in the field.

Upon passing the very table where Ms. Pennywhistle once lay, I shook off the image of her corpse bleeding at the knees. But there was one thing I could not shake off. On an adjacent work-table rested a mirror, one I used to check the deceased for fogged breath. In the mirror I glimpsed myself and did not recognize the man in the reflection. My auburn hair had turned white.

I climbed the stairs, fed the clothes into my fireplace, and watched my past burn. But I could never hide from it. For not only had events challenged my most firm beliefs, but they also marked me. I was now the man in white.

In my new official capacity as a witness to forces beyond our understanding, I, Milton Bland, hereby attests that the Woman in White to be as real as you or I. Some say the Woman in White wishes to save others from her fate. Even if her spirit is altruistic, I urge any with sound mind and body to barricade indoors upon the first sight of snow. For if ever one finds themselves as lost as I have been for the past five years, they too might encounter that which neither man nor woman were ever meant to see.

Time of death: six in the afternoon on December third in the year of our Lord 1785.
Time of life: eight in the evening on December third in the year of our Lord 1785.
~ so confirmed and signed by undertaker Milton Bland

All Aboard

Wilfred Culpepper awoke with a start and a bang of the head. Unsure if he was alone, he refused to curse out of courtesy, but his will to do so was strong. He rubbed the affected spot atop his head and sought to understand his surroundings. The world was dim and confined. Immediately, he felt a bout of claustrophobia settling in. Wilfred normally partook of much better accommodations than those he woke up in. He was also more accustomed to remembering when and where he bedded down for a night's sleep, but his memory was foggy.

A rocking motion (slight as it was) provided a clue. He was on a train. But how? When? Where had he boarded? Why was everything so fuzzy? And dark. Wilfred wished to light a lantern but was unfamiliar with his cabin that felt far smaller than those in which he normally travelled. Worse, there was no window. Never would he book a room without a window.

With no answers to be found where he stood, Wilfred moved into the hall. The clacking of the car on tracks and the low-level rumble of the steam engine verified his presence on a train. The corridor was empty of passengers, but with no idea of the time, everyone could have been sleeping.

Then a rear window caught his eye. Through the filthy glass, Wilfred spied an unfamiliar landscape. Tracks stretched out further than he could see, and thick forests lined both sides of the track. He was not in the city any longer, that much was certain. His presence in the last car bothered him more than the mystery of the destination.

"Absurd, I would never book a ticket in the tail car. There is trickery afoot, and I will not stand for it."

Filled with renewed vigor (and a growing sense of anger over his accommodations), Wilfred stomped down the length of the car and entered the next. The man's face turned red with rage. A supply car! It contained grain bags, crates of who knew what? And worse, passenger baggage.

Wilfred only travelled first class. Never would he ride near the tail, and more than that, never would he be caught dead riding behind the passenger belongings hold.

The day grew more absurd. Or night. The window earlier had provided a few clues to his situation. One, they were in the country. Two, it was dusk outside, the time of day when the world faded from light to dark. Wilfred reached for his pocket watch, intending to confirm the time, but found the pocket bare. Strange. Wilfred stepped into the next car filled with dozens of people crammed in narrow seats. They were a downtrodden looking lot. Nary a fur stole or gentleman's kerchief in sight.

"What is the meaning of this?" Wilfred asked himself, not the people crammed into the car.

Wooden booths of inferior quality lined the car. Some passengers looked Wilfred's way, but most stared off into space. (As confused as he?) There was no velvet to be found on the seats, much less padding. And there were no overhead lights to be found. But there were windows, and those kept the car from falling into total darkness.

No one responded to Wilfred's initial outburst, not that he intended for them to. Some passengers looked away, as if frightened by the angry man. Wilfred composed himself. Whatever was at play, it was not the fault of those without the means for better tickets.

"I apologize for my outburst, but I am rather perplexed by my whereabouts. Can anyone please inform me of where exactly we are travelling to?"

Everyone remained silent. Wilfred searched the eyes of the passengers, all of whom turned away when his gaze fell upon them. Most turned their heads toward the windows. Something about the windows in the car unnerved him, but Wilfred failed to identify the source of his discomfort. He turned his ire back to the passengers.

"What of it? Are you all daft? I asked a question."

A man in the corner, one in ragged clothes, trousers torn at the knees, standing near the exit door, cleared his throat. The man fiddled with a finger on one hand as if seeking a remedy for a hangnail. The man appeared in his thirties but was weary beyond his years. Tired, like all the other passengers. Without looking Wilfred's way, the man spoke up.

"Have at it then," the man said.

"Pardon me?" Wilfred asked.

"I shall not. Someone here will eventually respond to your belligerent inquiry if only to quiet the chatter. You will then berate any individual daft enough to help. Then you will demand to speak to someone else. That's what your type does. So have at it. Move on to the next car and squawk all you want but leave these poor travelers alone. They seek only peace, not your foolishness."

Wilfred stormed forward, insulted at the brazenness of a stranger of such low stature speaking to him that way, but the other passengers appeared amendable to the ragged clothed gentleman. Wilfred understood his instinct to throttle the man might not go as intended were the masses to disapprove. Instead, Wilfred latched onto something the peasant said.

"My type? There were others?" Wilfred asked. "Which way did they go?"

The standing man jerked his head to the door, but before Wilfred could step through, the ne'er-do-well implied a threat. "Beware the ticket taker."

"Pardon?" Wilfred asked, but decided it was not worth his time.

Wilfred left the man for the next car, which was alive with activity. The chef's station. Staff bustled about in the tight confines and cooked up a storm. Root vegetables and shoulders of meat lined wooden prep stations. The finest cast metal pans sizzled on controlled fires.

Claustrophobia struck Wilfred again, and he felt the desire to flee. There were too many people moving about. Never had he set foot in a train's kitchen, only ate that which such cars produced. Fearful the staff might misplace his hide for a side of beef, he navigated his way to the exit ahead. Unlike the forlorn folks in the last car, the kitchen staff were doing honest work at a pace that would make any employer proud.

The next cabin was as expected the dining car. Though compact, it was elegant, with sparkling white tablecloths and soft lighting from well-placed lanterns. All diners had dressed to the nines. Proper attire for public transport, Wilfred thought. The unfamiliar had become familiar. He took train trips for business many times.

Funny how he still could not remember boarding, though. Such a memory lapse disturbed Wilfred, who focused on something the man in a previous car had said. There were others like Wilfred, men of means, perhaps a gentle lady in their midst. Perhaps amidst celebrating a business deal with those in his circle back in the city, too many pints passed lips.

Not one to imbibe often, Wilfred could have easily succumbed to the liquid spirits. Though embarrassing, behind it all was a celebration worthy of excess. Shame Wilfred could not remember the grand deal that landed him on a train. Surely his fellow celebrants had fun placing him in the last car and waiting for him to wake.

If his friends were onboard, they were not currently dining. Wilfred recognized none of the passengers and they paid him any mind. His fellow compatriots had to be somewhere. But if they remained in their own sleeping cars (with far better accommodation than his own) he might never find them.

Wilfred planned to seek a familiar face, even if it meant walking all the way to the steamer engine. The vagabond he spoke to earlier warned of a ticket taker. It was an odd thing to warn someone about. Wilfred hoped to find a ticket taker. Such a person would likely know when Wilfred boarded and under which circumstances. Yes, Wilfred desired to find the ticket taker.

Or did he? A shiver ran through him at the thought. There was something in his memory that gave him pause. (A flash of lucidity?) But why should a ticket taker worry a man of means like himself?

Because of his missing stopwatch. Wilfred checked all his pockets. No ticket. Clearly, he had one if he boarded. Or did he? Was Wilfred a stumbling drunk stowaway? Was it possible? Did the joke begin and end with friends tucking him into a bed on a train without a ticket?

One way to find out. Wilfred moved to the next car, a passenger car, one where diners waited for seats to open in the dining car. Again, properly dressed, most were. A decent-looking lot, albeit all too happy to ignore him as well. One woman smiled and headed straight for Wilfred. She was lovely. It was as if she knew him.

But the woman bypassed him close enough to touch. Wilfred turned and saw the man she properly greeted. A fine-looking chap with his hair parted properly and his suit crisp and dry. A good-looking couple they were. Wilfred nodded to them in apology for stumbling into their space, but they were too involved with their meetup to pay him much mind.

Wilfred moved on, entering the bar car next. A rowdy lot sat in one corner, giddy with pints half empty. Wilfred knew if his friends were on board, they would likely find their way to a pint at some point. Wilfred took up a stool by the bar and signaled to the bartender before remembering his empty pockets.

With no cash in hand, Wilfred waved the bartender off before even ordering, but he maintained his spot at the bar. As Wilfred searched for a friendly face, he instead found a frantic one. A man burst into the bar from the next car. The man seemed frightened or confused. Feelings Wilfred understood all too well. The man was much younger than Wilfred, maybe in his twenties. Wilfred whistled.

The whistle startled the young man who, nonetheless, made his way over and leaned onto the bar alongside Wilfred. "Did you see him?" the young man asked Wilfred.

"Who?"

"The Ticket Taker?"

"No, but when I do, I have an earful to give about my accommodations," Wilfred said.

"I would not do that. You had better have your ticket ready if you encounter him. And pray you don't."

Wilfred frowned. "I am at a loss to understand. Quite the reputation he has. Why so worrisome a man?"

The man frowned back. "What I would not give for a pint. Calm my nerve before I tell you why. I have plenty of tales to share."

"Well, I have time. It seems I have lost my friends. And a stopwatch, wallet, and ticket. Wilfred Culpepper at your service. Mercantile specialist."

"Jasper Badger. Reporter."

"Explains the fancy clothes. A bit dandy they are."

Jasper looked down, as if noticing his too tight suit and puffy white shirt for the first time. He then slapped at his own pockets. "My overcoat. I was in the woods. It is frigid out there. Why would I leave it behind? Bah! The Ticket Taker. Spooked me, he did. I must have left the coat on a seat wherever I came from."

"And where did you come from? You do not strike me as a city boy, despite your attempts at playing privileged."

The lad settled some, surprised at Wilfred's observation if not candor. "Maybe you should be the reporter. Yes, I am from the city but cannot say that is where I truly belong. I am originally from the country. I escaped to the city as soon as I was old enough, eager to leave a dreadfully frightful place."

"Where might that be?" Wilfred asked.

"Our destination. For I know well the glen passing by through the windows. We are on our way to Sleepy Hollow."

"Why would I board a train to Sleepy Hollow? Absurd, I have no business there."

"Nor should you. It is known primarily for one industry, its restless spirits. I lost my teacher to one of the many legends of the hollow. Ichabod Crane, a worldly gentleman. Looked much like a bird and sang accordingly. I thought my time there was done. I wished to leave the very day I saw the headless horseman."

"Headless horseman?"

"Yes, eternally searching for his head, lost in battle."

"Bah! You sound like my wife. She belongs to societies of ill dispute, all of which believe there is more to this earth than the physical. Gibberish all. Free Masons, the Illuminati. There is no disreputable group she refuses to join. Nor does she refuse them services of various types up to and including the contents of my wallet. I humor her, but I refuse to listen to her chatter."

"A female allowed in such ranks? Unheard of. Those are closed societies, exclusive, predominantly male. My newspaper hears whispers of such groups. Even your wallet would not break such barriers. Your wife must possess an otherworldly knowledge beyond that of normal man to gain access."

"Well, she is quite lovely if you must know," Wilfred said.

"That matters not to such groups. No, their interest would lean more into that of my very own missing teacher. Witchcraft fascinated Ichabod Crane. Perhaps your wife has such knowledge or experience. She is correct about there being more to this earth than we know. I witnessed unexplainable events tied to a book of spells. Not to mention the Ticket Taker."

Jasper looked back once more, shivered, and turned pale. (Or was he always pale?) Jasper gulped and reached for a drink that was not there before looking around the car, confused.

"A mirror, there was a mirror earlier..." Jasper said, fading off.

Wilfred pushed away from the bar. "I have had enough. I demand answers. A ticket taker is but a mere employee. As such, there will be a master, that is who I seek. Despite your odd concern related to the ticket taking employee, I refuse to wait for answers any longer. I demand to speak to the man."

"Man?" Jasper whispered.

"Get some sleep, sir. You look like the very dead. I shall get my answers now," Wilfred said.

Bidding the confused young man goodbye, Wilfred moved to the next car, this one filled with more passengers who appeared to be seasoned travelers. Nothing out of the ordinary. Many read newspapers, maybe the very one the strange lad wrote for, Wilfred thought.

"Has anyone seen the ticket taker?" Wilfred called out.

Before anyone could answer, Wilfred had already entered the next car. Besides, the question had been rhetorical. Wilfred sought to find either the ticket taker or his missing (and mischievous?) friends. Eager to find someone, Wilfred sped up the pace. A passenger in the next car jerked with surprise when his open newspaper fluttered as Wilfred passed. The passenger sought the source of the commotion, but Wilfred was already gone.

Upon entering the next passenger area, Wilfred called out. "I demand the ticket taker. Has anyone seen the ticket taker?"

With the same blasé rudeness as earlier, most ignored Wilfred's cries save for one woman. She was an odd-looking sort who stood behind a curtain near the car's rear. (Was she hiding behind it?) She answered him by pointing toward the next car. Finally, Wilfred was getting somewhere.

Wilfred called out to the remaining passengers as he headed toward the exit. "It appears manners stayed behind at the last stop." He turned to the woman behind the curtain. There was something off about her, but he had neither the patience nor the interest in determining what that might be. "Thank you for the information. kind gentlewoman," Wilfred said.

The woman pulled the curtain tight as a cocoon. Once cocooned safely, the fabric shook as if the woman were freezing in the coldest of winters. Poor thing became separated from her coat, Wilfred thought as he entered the next car. Once there, he stopped short and fell silent. It was a sleeper car. Though frightfully impatient, Wilfred did not wish to wake those deep in slumber. He had just chastised fellow passengers for their lack of manners. It would be poor form to disturb anyone sleeping soundly.

Wilfred passed through a sleeper car, then another. Each was dimly lit, with only a few lamps stationed along the walkways. Even the ambient light in between cars from outside had faded toward darkness. There would only be so many sleeping cars before the train gave way to its engine. In the next sleeper car, Wilfred stopped as something in the distance caught his eye.

A most curious sight awaited him in the form of a tall man stooped over at the end of the car. His shape resembled a question mark. At first, Wilfred assumed the figure was nothing more than a shadow, but shadows did not move, and the thing at the end of the car did. It was difficult to attach a shape to the figure.

Thin, obscenely so, that much was certain, and something about the the way he leaned forward seemed unnatural. Then it dawned on Wilfred that he could not see the stranger's head! The man was nothing but bone. His ticket taker outfit rested tight against his body. With limbs so long, the man's pants could not contain the legs. The pant legs rode high on the man's calves, revealing skin pale as milk.

Finally the head made an appearance, which relieved Wilfred, who chuckled to himself. Wilfred felt foolish for allowing the young reporter in the bar to get into his mind with stories of a headless horseman. The ticket taker did, indeed, have a head. It was only because the man had leaned into a room at the end of the hall that Wilfred did not see it at first. But the relief proved short-lived. A better look at the individual caused Wilfred to gulp.

The man was sizeable, not in width or girth, but immensely so in height. The man wore a workman's cap (see he had a head) that nearly touched the ceiling because he was so tall. Initially, the employee took no notice of Wilfred. The man leaned into another room where he once again became a stooped question mark, as thin as assembled tree branches.

As unnerving as the man's tall, thin frame was, something else about the scene bothered Wilfred. Then it dawned on him. The train employee never opened a door, not the second or the first.

All doors in the corridor remained closed and yet the man had looked inside several as if he had passed through them.

"Impossible!" Wilfred cried out.

The cry drew the Ticket Taker's attention. The tall man pulled out of the room he searched (searching for what?) and finally noticed Wilfred. Wilfred assumed the dim lanterns impeded clarity of vision, for the man's features appeared like those of a ghoul, not a service employee. Wilfred gasped at the sight and shook his head. But the image did not go away. In fact, it became clearer as the Ticket Taker stepped forward into nearby lantern's cone of light.

It was a purposeful move, one designed to give Wilfred a clear view of the Ticket Taker. And what a view it was! The man's grin showed all his teeth, including molars. His skin was paper thin, especially on his face, where it appeared nothing more than fragile tissue paper wrapped around a skull and clipped somewhere behind his ears. His nose was non-existent, little more than twin cavities hovering above stretched lips. The man's eyes were sunken pools of black. It took the reflection off the lamp's light to confirm there were even eyes in the sockets.

"Ticket pleasssssse," the Ticket Taker said.

The word please came out like that of a snake. Not truly a hiss, but more like air escaping through gritted teeth that never seemed to open when the man spoke. The voice was authoritative enough that Wilfred instinctively reached for his empty pockets.

"My pardon, I am out of sorts. My watch, my possessions, I'm afraid..." Wilfred started, suddenly cowed under the height of the dark suited thin man who now stood midway down the car. When had he moved?

"Ticket pleasssssse!"

The ticket taker moved closer. Wilfred swore the suit was no suit at all, but part of the man's skin. If it was fabric, its maker had spun it finer than silk. The garment moved as one with the man's body. With legs that long, the man moved fast.

"Ticket pleasssssse!"

"I, uh, I... demand to speak to your supervisor," Wilfred whispered, unable to find his legs or his voice.

With thunderous steps, the man charged toward Wilfred incredibly fast. The cabin shook under the man's footsteps. Wilfred silently prayed passengers would wake and burst into the hall. Why? Perhaps to come to his rescue? But rescue from what? Wilfred surely owned a ticket stashed somewhere.

"Ticket pleasssssse!"

The man had picked up speed, was his own locomotive. The grin never faltered, but Wilfred did. He ran, in fact. The car shook underfoot as he went, violent enough he feared he might fall while escaping back the way he came. Once close enough, Wilfred launched himself through the door to the next car and collapsed to the ground.

Absurd! He felt absurd, there on his knees in a train car. The only reason Wilfred refused to cry out in indignation was a desire not to wake passengers who paid for sleeping accommodations. Those accommodations did not include blundering passengers such as himself. It surprised Wilfred that no one stuck their head out to check on the commotion. Wilfred would have welcomed the company.

Too stunned to rise, Wilfred turned over onto his back until facing the door he had just stumbled through. Made mostly of wood, the door contained a window of frosted glass on its upper half. Behind it, a shadow loomed.

The door burst open and the man, all limbs, bone, and unwavering teeth, stepped through the opening which appeared too small for him. The man filled every inch of the door frame, navigating through it one spindly limb at a time.

"Ticket pleasssssse!"

Wilfred scrambled back on his haunches. The Ticket Taker towered over the fallen passenger. Wilfred understood at that moment what had frightened the others so. A ticket would not appease such a horrid approximation of a man.

A ghoul.

That word struck Wilfred. His wife occasionally blathered on about such things, given her preoccupation with the mystical. Not one to pay much attention, her mention of ghouls unnerved Wilfred. His wife raised the subject at the dinner table, of all places, some months back. To end the inexplicable fear it prompted in him, Wilfred demanded on the spot that his wife cease the morbid conversation.

Perhaps he should have paid more attention, Wilfred thought. For it appeared the Ticket Taker was more ghoul than man. Wilfred rose and ran for the next car with the ghoul close behind! The ground shook as before, but sleeping passengers slept on. Wilfred cried out for their help, hoping to wake anyone, but every door along the way remained closed. Wilfred's heart thumped as violently as the floor underfoot.

"Out of my way!" Wilfred screamed, though there was no one blocking the way.

The fleeing passenger simply wished to have a clear path to escape a monstrosity whose movements thundered louder than that of a steam train hurtling along a track. Wilfred burst into another sleeper car and wailed to wake the dead. No one came to his aid.

Wilfred wondered whether the helpful woman from earlier was still hiding behind a curtain. He would soon find out. Maybe she hid because she understood the Ticket Taker was to be feared. Together, they could confront the ghoulish man and end the craziness. But Wilfred needed to reach her first.

Deep down, Wilfred appreciated his pursuer's single-mindedness, the dedication to his job. But further down in the places Wilfred's mind feared to tread, he worried that if he admitted to having no ticket, it might be the last confession he ever made. Wilfred ran.

"Behind me, he's behind me!" Wilfred yelled upon entering the overflowing car.

The woman remained tangled up in a curtain. She peered out of the fabric, nothing but eyes tangled in cloth. Hers were as fright-filled as Wilfred's.

"The Ticket Taker?" the woman asked.

Wilfred answered by gesturing to the other riders. "A ghoul follows close behind! A true living ghoul. Or are ghouls alive? Never mind, one is on my tail. I need help, good people!" None looked up. "Are you all daft? A person of distorted proportions and uncommon pallor angrily follows close behind. He threatens to throttle me at the least, but truthfully, I feel his intentions are more dire. I require help from every able-bodied man!"

The Ticket Taker's face filled the window at the end of the car. His ghoulish face pressed against the glass searching the car's interior. The horrific figure failed to notice Wilfred right away because there were too many riders in the car.

"He seems disinterested in the other passengers. That is why everyone remains so calm. They have tickets. The ghoul knows he punched theirs already," Wilfred said, feeling frightfully alone despite the sea of passengers.

"Ticket Taker?" the woman asked.

"Hurry, there is no time to waste. Before he sees us, we must go. Stay low."

Wilfred crouched and made his way to the end of the car, the woman in tow. She mimicked his movements, but her legs shook the whole while. They ran through the next passenger car.

Passengers were drifting off to sleep, unaware of the danger at their rear.

"Not for nothing, but a ghoul fast approaches. But sit there, ignore the peril. A sorry lot of cowards you are."

Another person buried in his newspaper looked up as his paper fluttered, but like before, Wilfred was already gone. This time with the woman at his heels. If the young reporter had not left the bar, he would be in the next car. The man, while a bit confused, mentioned the Ticket Taker as well. There was strength in numbers. Wilfred and the woman entered. Jasper was there, still leaning against the bar.

"I found the Ticket Taker," Wilfred said.

"And lived to talk about it. Ha!" Jasper said. "In your absence I discovered another mirror, confirmed it all."

"Ticket Taker," the woman said, still shaking.

"You knew about him, spare no details. Who is the foul man? What is his purpose?" Wilfred asked the man.

"I think I know now," Jasper said. "I am an investigative reporter. Do you know that?" Jasper asked.

"You mentioned, yes, but have offered me nothing informative. Will you make me wait for it to hit the newspaper before you fill me in?"

"What is her name?" Jasper asked.

"Cannot say. She is quite terrified of the Ticket Taker, that much I know."

Jasper looked the woman up and down while Wilfred glanced back at the door through which they came. Where did the foul man go? Turning from the window, he gazed at the passengers who sat so calmly. Wilfred felt suddenly silly. A man of his means and stature allowing an employee to frighten him so? Other passengers were calm, so why wasn't he?

Wilfred glanced back at the window as the Ticket Taker slammed his face against it. Glass shattered and the monstrous being reached through and grabbed Wilfred by the lapel. Wilfred wiggled out of his coat and raced to join Jasper and the woman who were already fleeing to the back of the train.

Wilfred long had issues with his heart because of consumption, the only misfortune to being fortunate. He worried his heart might give out while fleeing, but he ran. The ghoul moved like a locomotive behind them.

The trio fled through car after car but were running out of them. If Wilfred's memory served, they would soon arrive at his own sleeper car. Perhaps there he might find his ticket. The trio burst into the last passenger area before the supply car. Wilfred recognized the forlorn faces. Unlike the previous cars, everyone noticed Wilfred and company's frantic entrance. Jasper gestured to the crowd. Before he could say a word, the woman finally found her voice.

"The ticket taker!"

The passengers rose from their seats, gasping with fright. Wilfred was grateful to find the bunch (as downtrodden as they were) amendable to worrying over their plight.

"Finally, some brave souls. It took those relegated to the rear of a train to step forward with fire in their hearts. There are more of us than there is of him. I say we fight!"

All the people dropped back into their seats simultaneously as if a puppeteer had cut their strings. The sight startled Wilfred, who turned to Jasper, confused. Jasper nodded.

"I remember now. Against my good sense and wishes, my newspaper assigned me to revisit the Hollow. Having escaped years ago with my head intact, I should not have returned. Last I knew, the Headless Horseman had found a replacement for atop his shoulders. But perhaps like jack-o'-lanterns, the head eventually goes to rot. Perhaps he needed a new one, and I was there."

"What are you going on about? Why has everyone sat? I did not wish to proclaim such a thing, but I declare myself a man of means. My wife is an illuminati member. I offer a substantial reward for those who stand and fight. Who is with me?"

Sunken eyes collectively sank further throughout the cabin. The group was a defeated lot, and rather than Wilfred inspiring them, they shifted further back into their seats. Wilfred felt a rumble in his chest. Vibrations from the train or the oncoming threat?

"Do you know there are no longer undertakers in Sleepy Hollow? A funeral director, a caretaker for an overflowing graveyard as well, but no longer are investigations of foul play performed in the Hollow. Seems an undertaker mistook a woman for dead years ago. The undertaker was a farmer, one good with a hoe, but unreliable with a corpse. Now city elders send citizens suddenly unencumbered of spirit to the city for proper handling," Jasper said, as if in a fugue.

"I am from the city. I know well how such things work. What does it matter if this Sleepy Hollow sends their dead across the border? Why cannot you focus on the threat at hand?" Wilfred asked, getting into the face of the young man.

"In the late hour, all windows have become mirrors," Jasper said and pointed toward the nearest.

Wilfred followed the man's gaze and yelped. For there in the window, a reflection showed Jasper standing same as he was in the train, but minus a head! Wilfred leaped away from the man and cried out. He looked away from the reflection version, back to the real thing. Jasper still possessed a head.

"What trickery is this?"

Wilfred looked at the other windows and witnessed that which men were not meant to see. A scream rose in Wilfred's throat but froze as each new reflection stole a piece of his sanity. In one reflection, a portly woman in a tattered dress sat fully frozen, head to toe, covered in ice. Wilfred turned to the real woman, and she appeared fine. In her seat she was the same woman as in the window but not frozen.

Reflections filled every window in the long car. In each seat sat victims of untimely ends. Reflections revealed passengers with gashed necks, broken bones, bloated bodies, missing limbs, and other maladies.

One poor soul had a pitchfork buried deep in his stomach, or at least his reflection did. Combined, the reflections drove Wilfred to the edge of madness. The images were horrid, grotesque, and so... final. Then a thought came to Wilfred. There was one reflection he had yet to see.

His own.

Walking on wobbly legs, Wilfred approached the nearest window and faced the most terrifying reflection of them all. His own. It was his reflection, but not really. The mirror image showed a man clutching his chest tight, with a purple face locked in intense agony. The eyes (his?) bulged out so far that they threatened to roll out of the skull down to the floor. The reflection's tongue dangled from his mouth, long and thick.

Then, behind his reflection, another appeared over his shoulder. The Ticket Taker! The Ticket Taker whispered into Wilfred's ear with a foul breath that smelled like spoiled meat.

"Ticket pleasssse."

"I don't understand," Wilfred said.

But the other passengers were already on their feet and walking toward the last car on the train. Wilfred suddenly remembered which car engineers normally placed last on a train. The funeral car! Wilfred joined the procession and passed through the supply area before arriving at the very car from where he first awoke. Jasper held the door open for everyone as they passed through single file, too calm by half where Wilfred was concerned. The Ticket Taker was suddenly the least of anyone's worries.

"Jasper?" Wilfred asked, finally remembering the man's name.

Jasper jerked his head to get Wilfred moving. The Ticket Taker loomed behind them, waiting. Wilfred stepped into a car loaded top to bottom with coffins. Each passenger climbed into their own casket. Most were simple pine boxes. One coffin more elaborate than others sat off to one side. Jasper gestured to it.

"Fancy accommodations. You are a man of means. *Were*, I should say," Jasper said.

"What is this?" Wilfred asked, gesturing to strange markings atop the elaborate coffin in the corner.

Jasper stepped forward. "I read from a book years ago. One steeped in witchcraft. You say your wife was involved in the illuminati? Perhaps witchcraft is her true passion. I would dare say she has transcribed on your box a spell to ensure you walk again."

"Why bury me in Sleepy Hollow then? I have no connection there."

"Because that is where spirits go to roam. Perhaps she plans to reunite with you there. If not, she hopes it will be a place where you can find company. Maybe I will even see you there,"

Jasper said and opened his own casket nearby. "Or not. My head is indeed missing. If I were to roam, it would be difficult to see."

Jasper climbed into his casket and closed it. That left only Wilfred and the Ticket Taker. The ghoul grinned and gestured to the open casket. Wilfred climbed effortlessly, finally understanding why he could move so freely earlier. He had not a body to burden him, and no more pain in his chest to deal with.

Wilfred looked at his corpse in the coffin. Despite generous financial resources, the undertaker failed to disguise the frozen look of pain on Wilfred's face. Wilfred wished to escape, but there was nowhere else to run. He climbed into his coffin and found his body a perfect fit.

The Ticket Taker leaned in with a metal item that could have been a dental instrument, or a medieval torture device. It was neither.

"Ticket pleassssssse!"

With a thunk, the Ticket Taker used the hole puncher to punch a hole in a tag near Wilfred's foot. Then the Ticket Taker slammed the coffin closed. The train rumbled on until its next stop. Sleepy Hollow, where spirits with and without heads roamed the land.

THE CANDY HOUSE

COOPER PUT THE PEDAL to the metal, trying to make up time. His snot-nosed sisters threatened to rat out his planned day trip to their parents if he did not perform their chores before he left. His parents would have at least five conniptions if they knew he planned to bike all the way to the city to catch a movie rather than spend the day with friends, like he promised.

Tattletale scum-buckets he called his two sisters, but they did not seem to mind the burn. They played with their stupid dolls while he did the dishes and cleaned the bathroom on top of his own chores. Cooper believed one of them turded without flushing on purpose before he took over bathroom duty, though he could not put the offense past his father.

Luckily, his dad had already left for work, leaving one less parent to deceive. His mother was visiting the next-door neighbor, having coffee, and doing whatever grownups did. Cooper felt grown-up at fifteen, mostly, except his inability to drive landed him on the hard bummer side of life. No car left him feeling on the kid's side of manhood.

Movies were Cooper's life, and a new flick was his destination. His hometown of Tether Falls was small population-wise but dang immense in square mileage. Some properties sat a quarter mile from the next. Many parts of the town remained undeveloped. It was 1985 though. Times were changing. People were purchasing plots on which to build summer homes.

With people came growth, so Cooper hoped Tether Falls would eventually get its first movie theater. Such a thing would save him from all the pedaling. The nearest theater was in the city of Westbrook, many miles away. By car, it took almost an hour. By bike, on the back roads (his only option) it was about three.

Cooper had to (just had to!) see *Ladyhawke*. The new blockbuster had it all if the commercials were to be believed. The film starred Matthew Broderick, the awesome actor from *Wargames* along with Michelle Pfeiffer, the super-hot blonde from *Grease 2. She was no Olivia Newton John in leather*, Cooper thought, *but boy Michelle was all kinds of alright.*

Plus *The Alan Parsons Project* did the soundtrack. How cool was that? Cooper could not imagine how their music fit into an epic fantasy, but he was eager to find out. The only thing cooler would have been if John Williams scored the film.

Cooper had an Alan Parsons' song somewhere on the mix tape he played while pedaling. He always wore his Sony Walkman while biking. With so many miles ahead, each completed song distracted him from the effort and brought him closer to his destination.

"Gonna be your man in motion. All I need is this pair of wheels. Something, something, something—St. Elmo's Fire," Cooper sang along to the song on his tape.

This mix tape was his favorite because it was the one with the fewest DJ introductions to the songs. Cooper had gotten quite good at cutting the song intros out when he recorded them from the radio. The process meant missing a few bars of the tune, but it felt more like records (which he could not afford) without the blather of a DJ.

Many of the songs on Cooper's mix tape came straight from movies. Soundtracks were hot. Radio stations knew a good thing when they saw it. They played all the cool stuff, like songs from John Hughes movies, and even the grody disco Star Wars song.

The eleven-mile ride began near Tucker Road, shifted to a long stretch on River Road before segueing into several side streets before arriving at the city of Westbrook. Cooper had a beat to shit Schwinn ten-speed that he purchased at a yard sale.

The brakes were highly questionable. Rust covered the length of the cables leading to his tires, but the wheels were sturdy and fully inflated, so there were no problems there.

The gears were another story. The journey included many hills along the way, so shifting as needed would have been ideal. But from experience he knew shifting caused the gears to grind horribly which normally resulted in the chain dislodging. Getting the chain back in place was difficult and time-consuming. Heaven forbid he lose the chain far from home and have to walk the bike the rest of the way until his dad could fix it. Walking that far, even for Ladyhawke, was unthinkable. For that reason, Cooper left the bike eternally in fifth gear.

A matinee showing was key to his plans. Any screenings later in the afternoon guaranteed he would ride home in the dark. The thought frightened him. He had done so a few times, and each time vowed never again. But he kept breaking his promise to himself because the lure of the movies was too much. Plus, leaving on time remained elusive because sneaking out was hard, and his parents or sisters always delayed him.)

Riding at nightmare as he called it, was life-threatening. With no streetlights outside the city limits, he struggled to remain on the narrow roads he could not see. Homes were not plentiful on the route and most porch lights went off after a certain hour. Trees lined both sides of the country roads and their tall branches blocked even the moon and stars that might have helped light his way at night.

Sand became his radar. Sand was used to edge the pavement and over time it bled onto the actual blacktop edges. Cooper biked slowly at night which allowed him to hear the crinkle of loose particles crunching under his tires before he hit the actual dirt off to the side. As soon as Cooper felt or heard the crackle of sand he steered back onto the pavement. Besides being scary, night travel added an extra hour of commuting because of the slow pace.

Famed poet, Robert Frost, was a local. Cooper often thought of Tether Fall's streets as the 'roads less traveled' that Frost wrote about. Cooper hated poetry, hated English class, but boy did he love movies. He planned to move to Hollywood someday to make films, starting with a cool idea he had which involved introducing Indiana Jones into the James Bond universe.

"Jones, Indiana Jones," Cooper said loud enough to hear himself over the headphones. A song from the Rocky soundtrack played, sung by Rocky's brother. Who knew there was that much talent in one family? Cooper's mind wandered during his trips. But that was by design to keep himself occupied, especially because he neared a worrisome part of the route. There was no avoiding it. Not far ahead was the one thing that sometimes made him consider not making the trip.

The Candy House.

The damn Candy House.

The Candy House was an old home painted in an odd mixture of brown and peach hues touched off with rose pink accents.

Curved trimmings lined the roof's edges like frosting on a cake. The same frosting trim lined the porch rails running the length of the house. Cooper noted similarities to the house in Hansel and Gretel, where a witch lured hungry children to their doom. Once a kid entered her home, the witch would go all Julia Childs on their asses.

Rising three stories, the Candy House sat well off the road down a long dirt driveway which bisected an immense front yard. The home sat abandoned for as long as anyone could remember. Locals shared tales of a family that encountered something so frightening they left in the night without their belongings. Supposedly, an unfinished meal rotted on the kitchen table to this day.

Older kids interested in making a name for themselves sometimes planned to enter the abandoned structure. Yet none ever made it inside. Strange that Cooper thought. There were plenty of rabble rousers in town. There would not be a Tether Falls Correctional Center otherwise. Despite all the bragging about not being afraid, no one ever found the cajones to enter. None made it further than the front door. All who planned to enter abandoned ship without ever explaining why. Their silence in the aftermath of their missions only added to the mystery.

The house was up ahead. *Pedal fast is all*, Cooper thought. He needed to make up time anyway, or chance missing the early show. The house was coming up on his right. There were no other houses near the candy house. The isolated nature amplified Cooper's discomfort. If other homes surrounded the place, perhaps it would appear less menacing. Just another home odd enough to annoy the neighbors. The structure revealed itself through the trees, (which always seemed dead, shed of leaves even during the summer months). Cooper spotted the pink trim.

He remained in gear, wishing he could shift higher, but dared not lose the chain. Cooper focused on the road, trying to ignore the horrific home even as it rolled up on his right. Then a guttural groan filled his ears.

"Shit!"

Cooper slammed the brakes, skidding on the sand lining the asphalt's edge. He glided sideways into a stop. The skid angled him so that he faced the very thing he hoped to avoid.

The Candy House.

Too busy with his rescue mission, Cooper brushed aside his fear. In a practiced move, he hit the stop button on his Walkman and ejected the cassette tape. It had become gnarled in the machine. The guttural groan was the singer's voice slowing down as the machine ate the cassette tape. Cooper pulled the cassette out carefully, the crinkled magnetic tape stretching like spaghetti. It took the full reach of his arm to lift the cassette high enough to free it from the cannibalistic machine.

"Stupid batteries must be low."

They were always low. Higher priced batteries lasted longer, but he had little money and what he earned from chores he spent on camera film and developing costs for his Vivitar camera.

Though he longed to direct movies, he could not afford an 8MM camera. On his budget, all he could afford was still photography. He staged scenes with Star Wars toys, filming them in closeups as if they were real actors. It wasn't cinema, but the stills placed together told a story.

Cooper zipped open his fanny pack in which he kept his Vivitar stored with other trip essentials. A quick check for replacement batteries did not pan out. He forgot to pack any. Worse, he forgot a pencil. Without one, he had to use his finger to rotate the tape back in place. A laborious task. A pencil did the job much quicker. And the low batteries guaranteed the tape would keep being eaten.

Finished with the task, Cooper glanced up and spotted a bicycle leaning against the front porch of the Candy House. The bike looked old. A single speed with twenty-six-inch tires. Cooper was good with bikes, so he could identify that much, even from a distance. The J shape of the frame seemed old school, like the earliest days of bicycles.

From a distance, it appeared to be in remarkable shape after being exposed to the elements. If no one lived there, it meant the bike remained outside for years. His own rusty cables offered testament to what even a single winter in Maine could do to a bike. The Candy House bicycle tickled his brain with recognition, but he could not place what it reminded him of. The memory was like a sneeze that would not come.

Knowing the cassette would be eaten again without new batteries, he stashed his Walkman into his bag. While doing so, Cooper was overcome with the sense that someone watched him. That same feeling caused him to look up at the third floor. Goose pimples rose on his arms and neck. Then he leaped as something blasted in his ears. A pickup blaring its horn narrowly missed his rear tire. Someone riding shotgun tossed a Budweiser can at him. It missed and plinked along the asphalt.

"Get out of the road, Dingus!" the wordsmith in the passenger seat yelled while also using sign language via a raised middle finger.

Cooper's heart raced at the near miss, and the home started freaking him out again. It was only the unique bicycle that had kept him from riding away already, but enough was enough. Cooper decided he would take a picture of the bike and ask around to find out why it looked so familiar. Iconic came to mind, but Cooper did not really know what the word meant. He raised his Vivitar camera to snap a picture, but nothing happened.

"Totally bogus," he said and eyed the back of the camera.

Apparently, he had used up the film on his last Star Wars toy setup at the sandpit days earlier. With no extra film, he would have to skip the picture of the bike. He was freaked out anyway, so he placed the camera back in his fanny pack alongside the now unusable Walkman and tore off, racing away, happy to leave the Candy House behind.

Already on a tight schedule, the added delay of fixing the eaten tape caused Cooper to miss the matinee. That guaranteed at least part of the ride home would be in darkness. Cooper was not a miss the previews and the start of a movie kind of guy. He wanted the whole experience, which meant waiting for the next show.

While waiting, Cooper visited a nearby drugstore to drop off his film to be developed. While there, he purchased new batteries for the Walkman. As Cooper handed off the film for processing, he thought of the bike from earlier again. There was something about it. A fresh roll of film would allow him to snap a picture of the bike on his return trip. He had saved enough money for popcorn, soda, and candy. If he skipped the candy, he could maybe afford a new roll.

"What's your cheapest film for my camera?" Cooper displayed the Vivitar to the eighteen-year-old clerk.

"For that piece of junk, they only make cheap film."

Cooper deflated. It was the best camera he could afford. Film directors had to make do with what they had, right? He remembered they seldom showed the shark in Jaws because of budgetary constraints. Still, the acknowledgement stung.

"I just need to take pictures of a bike is all. Saw an old one on my way here."

"Does it have a chick on it flashing her tits?"

"What? No," Cooper said.

"Then I'm not interested in anything you're saying. Here, we have a sale on this off-brand. Knock yourself out with your bike pictures."

Cooper left the store as the movie was about to start. He rushed to the theater and during the previews loaded the new film since it was dark enough to do so. Before the previews ended, he also replaced the batteries in his Walkman.

"That was the best movie ever!" Cooper yelled on his way home. The sky had not fallen dark yet. The summer sun took longer to set than in fall, so he was lucky there. Still, full dark was imminent for part of the trip if he did not get a move on.

He wished to buy the soundtrack to *Ladyhawke*, but figured the record would cost a fortune. At least twelve ninety-nine. He would have to find a job over the summer since his birthday already passed and Christmas was super far away. No way could he wait that long for it.

The sky settled into grey as dusk settled in. Traffic was minimal in his town but plentiful in the city. Most vehicles already turned on their headlights, making it difficult for him to see whenever one passed him. Those same lights warned him he was running out of daylight.

His tape appeared okay on the return trip. While the batteries were new, the tape had yet to cycle through the spot where the machine ate it earlier. Sometimes a tape made it and was good to go. Other times, it would forever tangle in gears again at the same spot on the tape. The Sony Walkman Gods would either claim it for eternity or allow it to pass. The Candy House was fast approaching, so he turned off the tape and stopped out of view of the house to prep his camera and steel his nerves. He could not believe he wanted to take a picture of the place. Not so much the place, but the bike.

Cooper knew the bike from somewhere. He placed his Walkman in his fanny pack and readied the camera. After snapping a picture, he would ask his father about it. His father was old, maybe even rode the same bike when he was a kid.

Kicking off toward the house, Cooper grew increasingly nervous. He pedaled slowly. It was only because he was pre-occupied with rescuing the best mix tape ever earlier that he managed his fear of the Candy House. Though afraid now, he vowed to be as brave as Matthew Broderick in *Ladyhawke*.

All he had to do was man up, take the picture, then run. Cooper pulled over near the Budweiser can from earlier and felt a sense of being watched again. Night was fast approaching, so Cooper lifted his camera and snapped a photo. The flash went off because it was dusk, but the artificial light was meaningless from such a distance. The only purpose the flash served was to remind Cooper things were getting dark. *Time to get a move on, cowboy,* he thought.

After taking the picture, something caught his eye high in the house. On the third floor, he swore something flashed in a window. It could not have been his camera; he was too far away. But something bright popped in the same window from which he felt watched from. A curtain appeared to drop back into place. Was someone up there?

Cooper snapped another, which created a new echo flash from within the house but one story lower. There, on the second story, another drape fell into place. Cooper thought he glimpsed a woman before the top floor curtain moved. This time, he was certain. But no way could anyone get down a flight of stairs that quickly, especially an older person. *One way to find out*, Cooper thought.

With shaky hands, he raised the camera and snapped another picture. A light echo did flash on the first floor, but there was no motion behind the curtain this time. But there was something far, far worse. Cooper looked at the old bike and screamed!

The woman from the windows was sitting on the bike! The old bike no longer leaned against the porch but faced him with a rider on board, arms raised high on the handlebars. Now Cooper remembered why the two-wheeler looked so familiar. The woman resembled Miss Gulch from the Wizard of Oz.

Miss Gulch was the neighbor who became the Wicked Witch of the West in Dorothy's dream. Miss Gulch rode the bike before turning into the witch and riding away on a broom. The image always haunted Cooper. She resembled Miss Gulch right up to the empty cage basket on the front. The woman rose off the seat and pedaled. Despite the steep driveway, she effortlessly gained momentum, riding straight toward him.

As she drew closer, it became clear she was not Miss Gulch at all, but looked very much like an actual witch. All the way to a face covered in heavy, dark-green face paint. The woman flashed a wicked smile, exposing white teeth outlined by black lips that matched eyes as dark as coal.

Cooper turned his ten-speed in the homebound direction, knowing a ten speed versus a one speed would clear him away from the crazy lady in no time. He cranked the pedals and skidded from dirt roadside onto the pavement. But glancing over his shoulder, he saw that the woman never merged onto the road.

Something clacked against his bike frame so loudly it startled Cooper enough that he almost crashed. But the source revealed itself when he looked down. With no time to store his camera away, it remained in his grip, dangling from a nylon strap. The body of the camera bounced against the metal frame as he sped down the road. He would deal with it later. Cooper wanted to ride a safe distance away before stopping to store it.

At the speed she pedaled, the woman should have already hit the road. Cooper glanced back and was relieved to find the pavement behind him clear. That meant she must have stopped at the driveway's edge. For a moment he wondered if she ever existed at all.

The Candy House spooked him so much he could have made it all up in his head. One sure thing was real, though. The bike was there on the earlier leg of the trip when he was not so frightened. In the light of day, there was a bike for sure. One that could have been a replica straight from the *Oz* movie. That explained why it looked so familiar.

Something crunched in the trees to his left. Cooper looked off the side of the road and cried out. About fifty feet away, the witch rode her bike through the dense forest! Despite pedaling across loam, mulch, and branches, she kept up with him.

Cooper watched her in profile as she somehow navigated the woods with no difficulty. Somehow, she rode the forest floor while mirroring his own flight. She wore a black hat, much like in the movie, along with a black dress with puffed out shoulders in the fabric.

The only difference from the film appeared to be her eyes. Those horrible eyes. They were deep wells that well could have been twin black holes rotating within impossibly deep eye sockets. Her snarl remained constant, the guise of one determined to outrace him.

Where was a passing car? There had to be one coming soon. Where were the bozos in the truck? Cooper prayed for traffic. He planned to ditch the bike and leap into the first vehicle that came along.

Worse, he had no turnoffs on which to lose her. The road ran straight for at least a full mile. The next turnoff would not appear until after the church (with the large cemetery in the rear). If he made it there, perhaps he could enter it safely and pray away the devil on his tail.

With a cackle, the witch threw her head back, delirious with the chase. At her current speed, she would soon catch him. While remaining parallel to him, she also angled closer to the road as she went. As slight as the angle was, they were heading into an intercept. Already she was less deep in the surrounding forest than when she started. Each time the woman appeared close to hitting a tree, she somehow managed her way around.

Cooper spotted a ray of hope ahead. A house appeared in the distance, one that interrupted the forest and blocked the woman's path. Finally, a house! Cooper knew many residents in Tether Falls but did not know any who lived on River Road. The house would force the witch to go around since it blocked her path. The forest gave way to a front yard before converging back into woods again just past the home.

He sped up. Though growing tired, Cooper hoped to lose her at the house. She was so focused on him, maybe she had not even noticed the oncoming structure. They were almost there. She tracked him so perfectly that he imagined a rope tethered them together. But a game changer neared. Cooper still had a straightaway while the evil woman faced a two-story Victorian directly in her path!

Cooper leaned into it, pedaling faster, ready to press his advantage. The woman ignored the path ahead and focused solely on him, as if completely unaware of the looming obstruction. She was about to pancake herself. The witch crossed over onto the lawn. Dew had settled with the onset of dusk, so water whipped behind her as she sped across the yard. Strange how she kept steady despite the slick surface.

Rising higher off his seat, Cooper pressed on like the bike racer at the end of *Breaking Away*. This was his chance to lose her. She approached the house and never even slowed, running straight into the side of the building. Cooper laughed.

Though terrified and much in need of a pee, Cooper yelped in relief. The old bat had ridden straight into the side of the house! He lost her. Or thought so until a cackling sounded from inside the house. The horrific laughter rose above the cacophony of crashing pots and pans, shattered glassware, and screaming residents.

The rider emerged from the opposite side of the house without ever slowing, still on his tail! All the lights turned on in the home. People inside yelled and cried out in surprise. Whatever went down in the house, it sounded like pure chaos.

How? How was she still after him? She rode the forest floor as if it were clear asphalt. Cooper gripped the uneven handlebars. The right curved grip of his ten-speed still had its original black foam wrap, but he long ago replaced the other side with black electrical tape.

A buildup of sweat soaked and loosened the electrical tape until it slipped off, causing his hand to slip off the handlebars. The bike shook as the handlebars wobbled. A bull trying to toss its rider. Cooper slowed while fighting to regain control. Gripping the exposed metal caused his hand to ache as he battled to hang on.

Tears streamed down his face. He had needed the witch to crash into that house, but she did not. He could not ride at the current pace forever. While he struggled to continue, she simply grinned through it all. Instead of looking ahead, she focused on him with the understanding he would soon run out of gas. She angled her trajectory ever so slightly toward the road.

Cooper eyed his gearshift. If he shifted into higher gear, he could outrun her. He understood the risk, but figured he had no choice. Reaching down, he flipped the lever, shifting all the way.

Ka-thunk.

Pain jolted up his leg as his foot slipped off the pedal and struck the blacktop, twisting painfully even while the bike continued forward. His pedals lost contact with the chain when he shifted.

"No, no, no!"

Cooper felt the bike give up the ghost, which caused the witch to cackle harder. So close now, so close. He got both feet back on the pedals and cranked out several rotations. The grind of the chain sounded like a chainsaw unwilling to start. The woman was gaining, and he was slowing down. Then suddenly the chain took!

He grunted at the extra effort the higher gear required. He had not used the upper speeds in some time. Despite the difficulty, he moved faster. But the witch sped up as well. Cooper burst into sobs.

Rivers of snot rolled from his nose, while tears flowed from his eyes. How could this happen? Why wouldn't she stop? Where was everyone? He needed help. He was so, so tired.

Cooper spotted the church up ahead. His church. The one he attended Sunday school at. It was as far into that side of town as he ever went with his family. He never ventured into Candy House territory unless sneaking away for the movies. He prayed he could reach the church.

The witch cackled wildly but appeared to notice the approaching curve. Not only was the church looming, but the wild turn in the road that fronted the religious building. Around that bend was a steep incline that ran downhill.

On the witch's side, another house sprung up, but she barreled through that one as well. Children screamed inside. More glass crashed as she passed through. A car alarm went off, blaring in the night. The road became hard to see as night settled in. Asphalt merged into shadows. Cooper could not afford to slip off the road. The bike would not absorb the same punishment hers appeared capable of.

"Go away!" he yelled.

Cooper finally stopped crying, too exhausted to shed more tears. He was ready to give up. His legs burned and cramped.

The witch closed in. He felt more than saw her angle toward him, ready to intercept. The ever-present knocking of the camera continued, an annoyance that any other time would have drawn Cooper's ire. The abuse took its toll on the device. Its strap frayed, threatening to give. Cooper could not worry about that now.

The bend approached, and the witch launched herself toward him. She used the upcoming curve to ride at him. She would catch him before he could get off the bike and into the church. His best chance was if he could ride straight to the door and rush in. If the church doors were even unlocked. *Churches stayed open for those in need, right*? He needed it to be open. Desperately needed it.

Moving in closer, the witch was almost on top of him. His higher speed suddenly meant nothing. She would not stop. There was only one chance, the ditch and run. But as he rocketed toward the curve, Cooper found his bike speeding up when he needed to slow enough to leap off. Worse, his hand began sliding off the exposed metal handlebar again. He was going to bite the dust if he tried to slow on the turn.

She was so close! He went into the turn and let gravity take over. The curve caused him to swoop so wide he almost rode into the front of the church in what would have been a horrific crash at that speed. But then he was riding the curve. The sharp turn swept the camera up in the centripetal force, causing the strap to snap. He felt the tug as the camera ripped itself from his grip.

The camera smacked into the ground and bounced away at the same time the witch caught up to him. Cooper ducked as her arm swung wide above him, the black cloak looking like a raven's wing. He heard its swoosh as it missed what may have been an attempt to sever his head. Cooper leaned into the handles, riding the hill, feeling his speed increase even as the world seemed to move in slow motion.

Then the strangest thing. The cackle followed the trajectory of the camera. He looked back and could no longer see the woman. The Wicked Witch was gone. Cooper rode the hill, allowing it to bring him home.

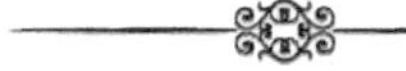

In the days that followed, Cooper's family worried after he refused to leave his room for an entire week. He claimed to be ill. Truthfully he was. Dehydration from the ride had taken its toll. He developed a fever and vomited for days. What Cooper refused to tell anyone was the true reason he puked was because of the flashbacks to that night.

In his mind, Cooper could still hear the cackle and see the raven-like wing of her dress sweeping near his head. When he closed his eyes, he saw her green face with ebony eyes.

The first Sunday after the incident, Cooper asked his parents to take him to church. He shuddered when they pulled into the parking lot. The scene reminded him of how close (so very close) it all came to ending right there. While it haunted him to return to the spot, he needed the comfort of strangers and a spiritual boost. His parents were happy to see him leave the house but surprised at his desire to return to such a familial Sunday tradition.

After the sermon's end, the preacher addressed housekeeping matters. The man mentioned upcoming suppers, Sunday classes, charity work and eventually something that shook Cooper.

"We found a camera in our parking lot last weekend. We assume it belongs to a parishioner. The strap broke, you may not be aware you lost it. If it is yours, please come forward," the preacher said.

Cooper did not claim it and never would. He realized the camera was the witch's true target. She did not want her picture taken. Maybe she could only go so close to the church, leaving her unable to retrieve it from the parking lot that day. If the camera remained in the building, she would have no way to get at it, or get at him.

He prayed the priest never opened the camera for inside near the spot to load film, Cooper had long ago affixed a sticker with his name on it. Cooper feared if the camera ever left the safety of the church, it might free the woman from the house once again.

Luck only takes one so far and Cooper felt he used all his luck up that night when the strap broke, and gravity took over. Deep down Cooper understood that if ever there was a next time, the witch would win the race.

ABOUT THE AUTHOR

PAUL CARRO IS AN active Horror Writers Association member and author of the acclaimed horror novels *The House* and *Abject Fear*. His short stories have appeared in multiple anthologies. He is editor and coauthor on The Little Coffee Shop of Horrors Anthology series. His screenplay *Penance* is set up with legendary film producer Michael Phillips. He is currently in development on the film and novel adaptation of *Hitchcock, Nebraska* as writer/producer. Horror flick director Rolfe Kanefsky is attached to direct. Paul has served as a producer/writer in film and reality TV, and resides in Santa Monica, California. When not writing Paul is hiking throughout the state.

ALSO BY PAUL CARRO

Scientists trying to cure fear must face their own when the groundbreaking experiment goes horribly wrong. In the race to cure fear there will be casualties. And blood. Lots of blood. Are you ready to face your fears?

"the horror sequences are delightfully grotesque..." —Kirkus
"Carro blends a conventional horror tale with an innovative, new concept... character backstories are incredible... intriguing and gory." --EbookFairs

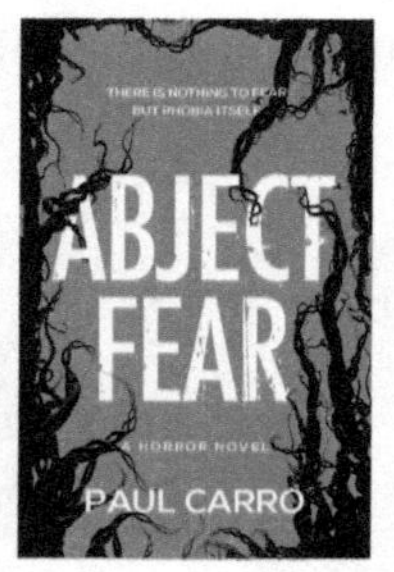

ALSO BY PAUL CARRO

The day began when Sheriff Frank Watkins discovered two bodies and three heads. Then things got strange. When a mysterious house appears form thin air in a field, the town of Tether Falls, Maine will never be the same. Doors open throughout town and people are transported into a terrifying world beyond their understanding. Soon residents find themselves trapped together. Nine strangers with nine secrets so dark they wish to take them to their graves. One house is willing to accommodate them all. Strap in for a pulse pounding horror thrill ride from acclaimed horror author Paul Carro. A member of the Horror Writers Association, Paul has created a terrifying world where nothing is at it seems. The House is now open. Enter if you dare!

ALSO BY PAUL CARRO & JOSEPH CARRO

2 authors from 1 family visited 12 coffeeshops to craft 12 single sourced cups of terror!

Authors Paul and Joseph Carro the only known uncle/nephew horror writing duo visited twelve coffeeshops around the country and used the location to inspire twelve unique tales of terror. Each story is prefaced by the coffee shop we worked in and what inspired us. Volume two even adds drink recommendations. If you love naked zombies. killer hill people, and aquatic horror, you will love The Little Coffee Shop of Horrors Anthology. Volumes 1 and 2 available now!